WAITING

WAITING

CAROL LYNCH WILLIAMS

A PAULA WISEMAN BOOK

SIMON & SCHUSTER BFYR

New York   London   Toronto   Sydney   New Delhi

SIMON & SCHUSTER BFYR

An imprint of Simon & Schuster Children's Publishing Division
1230 Avenue of the Americas, New York, New York 10020

For information about special discounts for bulk purchases, please contact Simon & Schuster Special Sales at 1-866-506-1949 or business@simonandschuster.com.
The Simon & Schuster Speakers Bureau can bring authors to your live event. For more information or to book an event, contact the Simon & Schuster Speakers Bureau at 1-866-248-3049 or visit our website at www.simonspeakers.com.
Book design by Lucy Ruth Cummins
The text for this book is set in Gill Sans.
Manufactured in the United States of America
2 4 6 8 10 9 7 5 3 1
Library of Congress Cataloging-in-Publication Data
Williams, Carol Lynch.
Waiting / Carol Lynch Williams. — 1st ed.
p. cm.
"A Paula Wiseman book."
Summary: As the tragic death of her older brother devastates the family, teenaged London struggles to find redemption and finds herself torn between her brother's best friend and a handsome new boy in town.
ISBN 978-1-4424-4353-2 (alk. paper)
[1. Grief—Fiction. 2. Family problems—Fiction. 3. Brothers and sisters—Fiction.] I. Title.
PZ7.W65588Wai 2012
[Fic]—dc22
2011043898
ISBN 978-1-4424-4355-6 (eBook)

FIRST EDITION

FOR
Michael and Cheri,
Hannah and Esther,
Brandon and Dianne.
Oh, how we miss you.

ACKNOWLEDGMENTS

There are always a million people to thank after the long process of writing a book. First cheerleaders for me are my daughters. I love all five of them! They believe in everything I write, even when I do not, and some listen to or read my stories more than once from first line to *the end*. With *Waiting*, Caitlynne was there from word one. This book began when a good friend of hers was killed. We have wept together over the past many months out of sorrow for the loss of a terrific person. *Waiting* is about grief—and Cait and I shared that, along with hope—during the writing of this novel.

I also want to thank Alexandra Penfold, my editor at Paula Wiseman Books. Alexandra has read over this book more times than I have. She's looked at every period, every comma, every line break, every space, every word. It matters to me that I have written the best story possible. I've never said to Alexandra, "I want to make sure every word counts," but she has known my heart and matched my vision now on two novels. I appreciate and love her for this. Some think that just publishing is most important. For me, publication with the right editor is most important. *Waiting* is what it is because my editor, Alexandra, cares.

WAITING

After it happened, no one in school would talk to me. No one. Not even my best friend, Lauren Hopkins, who has hair to her waist, and who let me dress like her until I figured out how to dress for myself.

She had said, "You know what, London? You homeschool types never look like the rest of the world. Even when you wear the right clothes."

(I had on blue jeans and a Billy Talent T-shirt and Vans, too. It must have been my face. It must have. A look. I've seen it myself in pictures. Wide-eyed, surprised. Happy.

But that's gone. That look is long gone.)

"So teach me what to wear," I had said, shrugging. Like I didn't care, you know? But I did. I cared a lot.

And while I didn't buy anything different from normal, she did show me how to use kohl eyeliner.

And that should be enough to keep you tight, right?

Clichéd.
So clichéd.
The whole thing.

Me sitting there, like I'm minding my own business. Eating a cheese sandwich from home. Just the right amount of mayonnaise. Swallowing, yes. But having a hard time with it. Like there's a fist blocking my throat.

The five chairs around me are empty because no one sits with me now. (Including Lauren Hopkins.) Maybe they're used to me being alone? Maybe they're afraid my tragedy will rub off on them? Maybe it's because I can't quite talk still? Whatever, they leave me on my own.

Lunchroom noises . . . Popping sounds of sodas being opened. Trays dropped on the table. Forks scraping on plates. Lunch bags being smushed closed.

The clichéd part is me on the inside.
I am ready to bust wide open. I feel it. I feel it coming up from the pit of my stomach, like a fast-growing foam. Like vinegar added to baking soda (and there's Zach pouring the liquid and saying, "People of Vesuvius, run for

your lives." And I'm laughing hard and so is Mom.). Like the feeling wants to burst out of me.

I'm the volcano.

For a moment I think, *Don't do it. Don't do it. Don't. Do. It.* That's how strong the urge to scream is.
The words *I didn't KNOW!* echoing in my head, the *o* sound going on, screeching toward the ceiling. Higher higher.

Will they look then? Will they even hear me? Talk to me? Sit next to me again? Leave me alone?

I hold it in, hold the scream back with both hands on my throat, tight, tighter, and it hurts. It all hurts. From the inside out. Tighter and tightest. Black in front of my eyes, no breathing for me.

The next clichéd part?
This new guy walks into the lunchroom and I gasp in air.

So I don't see him.
I don't see him.
I don't see him.

Second half of the day just about over. I walk the halls
alone. Check out the bathroom, make sure no one's
there. Lock myself in a stall. Take off my shirt, bundle it in
a ball, and scream right into an armpit.

Then when I come into English class late (even this is clichéd—I used to read. I know.), I see him, right there, sitting in the row closest to the windows. His long legs spread out in the aisle. He's grinning at what? Me? Can't be. I'm just here. Late and all, with a wrinkled shirt now that's wet from my scream and tears.

If my face would move, I'd smile. I'd laugh! Like before. I would throw back my head and let the laughter burst from me.
But I just step over his feet, notice his dark brown eyes, dark hair, and head to the last chair in the row next to his.

"London," Mrs. Pray says, "I'd appreciate you getting to class on time."

"Yes, ma'am," I say, not looking at her. Because I know what her face is. Full of sorrow for me. And after a screaming-into-my-shirt session, I cannot hold up under a look of sorrow. No way. That's too much.

Somebody snickers (about me?) and I stumble. Why do I have to care what everyone thinks? Why do I have to care that I'm alone?

At home, all life has stopped, even though it's been
a while. You think things get going again. And they do.
Sort of.

Here's how it works—
You become a shell. Fragmented. Soul seeping through
the bigger cracks.
You walk. Move. Arms into sleeves. Zip zippers. Run your
fingers through your hair. Swish mouthwash around your
mouth. Avoid flossing.

Nod when someone asks, "London, how are you?"
Look away when someone says, "I heard about your loss."
Want to tear skin with your teeth when someone says,
"Oh, he's in a better place."

You pass the closed door when you walk down the hall.
Wish things were different so we could sell. Move from
this house. Get away from here. Run.

Dad at work all day. More than all day. Sleeping under his
desk sometimes.
Drinking so much coffee that I can smell him from
across the room.

And Mom. On her knees. On her knees. Weeping into her pillow.
Looking the other way when I'm near.

"London?"

I look up from a stack of newspapers I haven't even read. Don't even know the name of the top one. I look only for stories of death. And nothing touches it.

"You're London, right?"

My eyes don't focus at first. How did she recognize me out of school? What was I doing? Nothing? Just sitting here? I nod.

She sits next to me. "Can I sit with you?"

She's in the chair. Why does she ask? I want to say that, be my old sarcastic self. Instead, I think shallow sarcastic thoughts that are only half feelings, really, and nod again.

"My name is Lili." She holds her hand out for me to shake. I don't. She drops her hand. "I just moved here with my family. And I heard about you so I thought I'd sit here. Do you care?"

I nod a third time, then shake my head no. Meaning yes. I want this warm body next to me till she finds out and leaves. Like everyone else.

Everyone's the same, you know?
Even when they say they're different, they aren't.
I scare them.
No one wants what happened to me to happen to
them.
And I can't blame them at all.

"Oh good. It's hard to be in a new place. Especially this
close to the end of the school year. I'm from Utah. It
was cold when we left. And look at the weather here."
She holds her hands out like I'll see a sample of the
weather—Utah, Florida—on each palm.

I glance out the library window. The sun's bright today,
I squint. I hadn't even noticed. And I'm sitting in a
rectangle of light so hot that all the sudden my neck
starts to itch and I feel all sweaty under one arm.

Look at this. See it.
There are dead people everywhere. Not like in that movie. I mean, everywhere.
In real life. On the news. In the papers. In history books. In my life.
I cannot wait to get away from this.

So how do I? Get away, I mean?

Die myself?
Cause that much more grief.
Tear a hole open in the universe and just get the hell out of here?

Mom wouldn't like it that I swear. She hates it when we do. I mean, when *I* do.
Or maybe not.
God expects more, is the whisper in the back of my head.

Well, the truth is, so do I.

A missionary's kid can't kill herself. It's against all the rules. It's against God's law.
But
But would He stop me?

Would Jesus come here, right here in this library, if I was getting ready to off myself, and stop me?
I didn't think so.

So I just have to stick around. No matter how I struggle to breathe. Be part of the plan. Part of the deal. Why?

Because accidents happen.

My whole family is aware of that.

Lili is settled all around me. She has on shorts and a long-sleeve T-shirt with SONS OF HELAMAN MOMMA'S BOYS written across the front of it (huh?), and I don't even see her coat.

"It's February," I say. It's hard to get the words out, but I do. Like that's enough. But she seems to understand and smiles.
"Isn't that great? Back home there's snow *everywhere!*"
Her library books slide all over my newspapers, pushing one to the floor. I ignore it. She puts her laptop on the table. "I'm writing a book," she says, and I think of Daddy with his nonfiction, talking about our family Before and the travels and the people we met and missionary work. I think how he used to read every section out loud to all of us.

Before.

I look at Lili. She's talking, but I don't really hear her. Her teeth are so white, and when she smiles she seems happy. I wonder if Zach would have liked her.

Would you have liked Lili, Zach?

Here's how I know God doesn't hear me:

Daddy, my daddy the missionary, traveling us all around the country, all around the world, serving others.

Oh, what I have seen, what I have seen. Earthquakes, murders, orphans, flooding, people lying dead by the side of the road—the list goes on and on. And all that happening with us praying together, as a family, whole. All in a circle, holding hands, my daddy's voice piercing the ceiling and headed straight to heaven.

And not one thing changed.

"You're changing," Daddy said. "Maybe God isn't sweeping the world clean of injustice, but, London, you're changing. You're getting stronger. Learning more. Loving God with a fierceness no one would expect."

And Zach just nodded, wide-eyed.
He believed. More than me. Always more than me.
He held on to his faith, even through his sad times, his hard times.

"It's gonna be okay, London," Zachy said. "It's never what we think."

I remember it was a hot November night. Our first Thanksgiving in the South and here was this freak weather.

"It should be," I had said.

Zach slipped his arm around my shoulder and we sat there, quiet between us, for the longest time. Then he said, "I know."

Zach was right.

Daddy doesn't know. Mom doesn't know. But on those trips, I think I started wondering about a god that would let all this bad stuff happen. All of it so awful. I *was* changing. Stretching from my old religious skin. Feeling itchy with the worrying and the cracking free.

And just know this. You don't have to be the daughter of a missionary to know what's going on. Watch the news. Read the paper. Check online.

I told you so.

So when I was little, Daddy said, "God answers prayers through Jesus Christ." And I believed. One day, believing, I wrote this note to Jesus. It was like, Are you there? Check one box, yes or no. And I folded the note up small and set it on the bar in the kitchen. I spied around for a while, watching, to see. Left. Came back.

"What are you doing?" Zach said.
"Waiting," I said.
"For what?"
I couldn't say, "For Jesus." Or maybe, with Zach then, I could have. But I didn't. That's all I'm saying now.

I didn't.

Now with this company I don't look for a quiet
moment. In fact, there's nothing quiet about Lili. She runs
her mouth and never takes a breath, I don't think.

She's here, that strange Lili. Sitting up close, hands folded,
ponytail falling forward, leaning at me as she chatters.
Utah this and that, she says.
Grammy and Grampy this and that, she says.
And what about Disney World, it's waaaay better than
Disneyland, right?

Sure.

I look at her and stay quiet. I let out a sigh.
She can *talk*. Wow.

This talker saves me from having to speak.
This talker is better than being alone.

How did Lili happen upon me here at the library? I shift in the sun, glance at the clock. Forty-five more minutes before Daddy will pick me up.

"Tell me about your family," Lili says. "Do you have any brothers or sisters, London?"
Just like that. Like she has a *right* to know.

I swallow, swallow, look at her side-eyed, back at the clock. In the sun her dark hair has a red tint. She's thin, looks like an athlete. I catch my breath and there's time for my words because she's stopped talking. She waits. Quiet.

After the account of the long drive from Utah, after Provo High, after being the middle of five kids (four boys and her) and being an aunt when she was twelve, after how her father is the new football coach at the local university, after how her mother can't get bread to rise in the Florida humidity, she looks me right in the eye and waits for my answer.

That's an ugly question sitting on the books between us. "Do you have any brothers or sisters?"

My body takes over.
I'm up, going, headed toward the door. Leaving
everything behind.
I look back once, flip her the bird. Her mouth drops
open.

How the hell did she find me, anyway? All tucked away
in the back like that?

For a moment I imagined her as a friend. A good friend.

I could have lived with all the talking, turned my ears off,
nodded when I needed to, if I had a friend again.

But she is, I see, just like everyone else—wanting to
know the end.

Daddy beeps as he passes, makes a U-turn. Pulls up alongside me. I climb in the car.
"London, you didn't wait for me."

My mouth is dry as a sock and I'm cold. I want to say something, answer him, tell him what just happened, but my voice is trapped in a box.

Lili and her stupid T-shirt and shorts.

"Honey, I told you I'd pick you up. You've been walking a long while. You're halfway home." He sort of looks at me.

We pass a huge orange grove. This is why we live here now. After Daddy retired and decided to settle down in one place. We came here for the oranges and avocados and hot, steamy weather.

"Are you okay, London?"

I glance at my father. My eyes are dried out too. Now I'm hot all over, though my fingers remind me of ice chips. And I can't stop trembling.

"Let me get you home," Daddy says.

I open my mouth to speak, to say anything, but Lili
seems to have used up all the words I might have said
today.

She has four brothers.
Count them. One, two, three, four.

And my one is none.

When almost all the shivering has stopped, Daddy says,
"Honey, your mom's resting again today."
I look at my hands, empty of everything. Not one library
book, not even a magazine, though I'd thought of putting
together a stack on the table, if I hadn't been so tired,
and checking them out.

I stare at what might be the lifeline on my palm.

The truth is, books used to connect us.
They're something we always had, even in Africa, though
not like what's here in this house.
I can do without the books this weekend—I haven't
read anything I wasn't forced to in *months*. What I need
is to share the air with what's left of my family. Take small
steps. Sleep on the edge of life.

"I'm going back to the church to look over
photographs for this next book. I'll work in my office
some more."

Sunnyside Baptist Church opened its arms to us when
we arrived, because Daddy is a well-known missionary.
They wanted him here. Gave him an office to work
from. He's even spoken from the pulpit several times
over the past three years.

I mean, Before.
Not as much now.
He needs time.

When I glance at Daddy, I see he doesn't look in my direction. He grips the steering wheel. Holds tight. Stares ahead. Just stares ahead, hanging on to the steering wheel. Looks at the road like it's his best friend.

I bet it is. I bet the road *is* his best friend, because he has always loved to travel.

"Right," I say. I'm surprised I found my voice, like all along it was hiding in the backseat or near my lifeline or something. "Thank you for picking me up."

"Sure thing, honey."

We drive down our street, so green. Trees hunch over the road, cold sunlight splashing through, houses set far apart, wide spaces between, and a breeze moving American flags like a gentle wave, like they're saying good-bye to an almost-friend. A talkative almost-friend.

"I'll be home by dinner."

I nod.

We pull in the driveway. The house seems all closed up,
the windows dark-eyed. The sidewalk even feels like
it might roll up and pull the welcome sign off the tole
painting Mom did so long ago.

"Check on your mom for me, huh, London?"

When I touch the car door handle, a shiver runs up my
arm, makes me look Daddy in the eye.

For a moment we stare at each other.

Who would think someone could get old in just a few
short months? But it's happened to my father. His hair
graying like it is at the temples. Wrinkles that make
him look sad, even if he smiles. He just seems brittle
somehow. We all are, I know.

Then I see it. Past the age. Past the gray and sadness. I
see him—
Zach, my older brother,
hidden in my
daddy's face.

"London, come with me."

That long-ago night, my eyes popped open. Zach stood
over me, in his pajamas. His hair was all messed up from
being asleep. He was right in my face, so close I clapped
a hand over my nose to keep from smelling his breath.
He laid a finger on my hand like he was silencing me.
"Come on. You have to be quiet."

I got out of bed, clutching Mandy, my little one-eyed doll.
The wooden floor was cold.

"Guess what I found?"

"What?" My voice came out low and full of gravel.

"Shh!"

"I'm tired."

"You're going to like this. You will." He took my hand in his.
We went down the hall to Mom and Daddy's room. The
door was open just a bit.

Everything was gray. Even Zach. But the hall night-light
was a yellow blob with shadows spreading away. It
scared me, seeing it like that, but I didn't tell Zach.

"They're sleeping in there. So really shush now."

"Okay."

He pushed the door open. I could see our parents in

bed. He pulled me to the closet. Their big walk-in closet. Opened that door. Led me in. Closed the door. I could smell the leather of Daddy's shoes and Mom's perfume.

He flicked on the flashlight.

"Look." The beam of light circled the tippy-top of the closet. Christmas presents. Wrapped already. Way up there. "Santa's been here." He lighted the presents again.

"How do you know it was Santa?" My voice was a growl.

"Right there. See?"

I saw. FROM SANTA in black marker.

Zach flipped off the light. We stood in the dark closet. The space smelling of our parents. I felt disappointed. I had thought, well, that Santa *did* work at the North Pole. That he brought things from there on Christmas Eve. Not that he stored presents in my parents' closet.

I felt Zachy's hand. He tugged me out into the bedroom, out the door, back down the hall. He tucked me into bed.

"We won't tell them we know," he said.
And we never did.

Mom is in her room. I knew she would be when I stood on the front porch and watched Daddy leave.
I open her door, which is closed almost all the way, remembering that Santa night even though we lived in a different house then.

"Mom?"
She moves in bed. I can see she's lying on top of the covers. She's fully dressed, so that means she's been out. But she doesn't answer.
"Daddy wanted me to look in on you. Is there anything I can get for you?"
Nothing.
She hasn't spoken to me in months. Not when it's just the two of us. Not when Daddy is home. Not at all, not at all, not at all.

"He's put dinner on," I say.
Has she plugged her ears?
Does she hear me?
Do my words make their way to her?
I see her roll over, turn her back to me.

A part of me wants to run in there. Run in and shake Mom. Scream in her face. Make her SEE me. I touch my throat, squeeze my eyes shut. Turn around and pull the door to, leaving it cracked open just a bit.

I finish making dinner—glass pitcher of iced tea cooling in the fridge, brown-and-serve rolls ready to bake as soon as Daddy gets home, a Sara Lee pie pulled out of the freezer to thaw.

It's quiet here. Like I live all alone. The house breathes opposite me, breathing in when I breathe out. Presses its memories on me. If walls could talk, what would these walls say? Would they close their eyes to memories, like I want to?

When I can't stand it, I turn on some music, classical, so soft it can't be heard down the hall.

Sometimes, when it's late, really late, I'll pull out some of Zach's music. I hid his iPod when Daddy searched my brother's room for answers. I don't listen often. But on a night like this, maybe someone else's wailing will help me

out.

I dream he's alive.

He wakes me with a low, "London." I cover my face, hide my nose from his breath that is cold as frost. "I'm okay," he says. "I promise. Come with me."
"You're taller," I say.
He nods. "Maybe," he says. "Anything is possible here."
"Where?" I say. And I'm up, following him. "Where?"

I open my eyes when my feet touch the floor.
He's gone.

Zachy was so good-looking, even grown women did a
double take when they saw him.
His hair was blond (mine is sandy-colored with a
highlight of auburn)
his eyes so blue they made you think *fake* and
he was way taller than me, more than six three. He
might have kept growing forever if he'd stayed alive.

But the best part of my brother was when he was
happy, and he was, mostly—though there were times—
how he would throw back his head and laugh.

No one had a laugh like that.

Daddy misses dinner. Again.
(This never happened Before.)
Mom eats in her room with a bottle of wine I didn't
even know we had.

It's me
alone
looking at three empty chairs and wondering.

"Why do I even bother to eat?" I ask Zach's chair. "I can
hardly do it."
And that's true.
It takes real effort to lift the fork open my mouth chew
swallow breathe lift the fork open my mouth chew
swallow breathe lift the fork . . . you get the picture.

And if there isn't anyone to help by just being there, well,
what's the use?
So in the end I just eat a huge slice of Sara Lee pie.

"Before you get it, Zach," I say. My voice is a whisper, but
I can imagine him reaching for that pie, eating it from the
tin, and Mom laughing. "Before you hog it all."

I'm doing my homework at Zach's desk when the
phone rings.

(Right after, there were a lot of people who called.
And then they found out more and the calls stopped
coming. People didn't know what to say. At church they
wouldn't look any of us in the eye.)

It's weird hearing the phone ring.
I stand, step into the hall, and I hear Mom answer,
"Hello?"
Her voice is soft as warm air. I can almost see her in my
head, in her room in the dark, sitting on the edge of her
bed, hair a bit messy from lying down.
"Yes, she lives here."

She?
Me?

"Yes, I'll get her."

I stop walking.
She'll get me? She'll get me? That means, that means,
she'll have to call for me. I don't move. Can't move.

I can hear sounds coming from her room, but I don't volunteer anything. Just wait. Wait. Wait.

She says nothing.

I'm still.

I hear her settle on her bed.

My stomach is thin as paper.

After a while the phone starts that loud beeping sound, and I turn and go back to Zach's room, where I crawl under the desk and sit where his feet used to be.

"Jesus," our pastor says, "is the answer."
He says it to a room full of people. We sit in the front,
just me and Daddy, almost alone . . . except for the
Smiths at the far end of our pew. (People are afraid.
Don't look and it won't happen to you.)

Taylor Curtis sits in the choir seats opposite me here
in the congregation. Mom's not here. She quit church
months ago. Anyway, he's seventeen and has blond hair
and this big smile and eyes such a pale green that in
black-and-white pictures he looks crazy.

No one knows this except Zach—I mean he *knew* it—
but I think I loved Taylor before he decided he wanted
to be with Heather Nelson.

"I'll beat the crap out of him if you want me to," Zach
said. "Look at this." He showed me his muscles. Flexed.
Tried to make me laugh. "Long skinny muscles can pack a
punch. Want me to bust his butt?" They were friends, my
brother and Taylor. Good friends. On the football team
together.

"WWJD?" I had said.

"Probably send Taylor's soul into a herd of pigs that
would leap off a cliff and drown in the sea below."
I had laughed then, though I'd been crying before.

Now Taylor looks at me and he lifts his eyebrows,
something he did when we made out, like he's asking if I
want to meet him again.

No.
No. Way.
Even though kissing right now might make me feel
better. For sure would make me feel less lonely.

"He's right," Daddy says in a whisper, his hands folded
in his lap like he might be praying when he isn't talking,
and for a minute I think he means Taylor was right to like
Heather (it didn't last long). "Jesus *is* the answer."
Oh.
"He *is* the answer." And to hear him say it, why, I know,
I know, he believes, even if he carries the whole Castle
family belief on his own back.

Every day.
Every day is the same
is like the other

they run into one another
look alike.

I can't tell a Monday from a Thursday

only the sadness links me to them.

In school, in English, that beautiful guy is back.

I get there early to watch for him. Hurry so I can see him walk into class. And when he strides into the room, his jeans hitched a little low, that shirt open so anyone can see his throat, I know why vampires want to bite necks. My face colors at this stupid thought.

He's opposite of what I'm used to—of light-haired Taylor. He's dark-eyed, with nut-colored hair that's trimmed short. He's lean, not football hardened.
I can't stop looking at him.

"Hey, Jesse."

It's Lauren Hopkins. She's run in after him, linked her arm with his, and now she slides down the aisle with him. He glances right at me, just for a moment. Shows a bit of his teeth in an almost-smile. Then looks down at her.
"Hey," he says, and I'm not sure if he's talking to me or to her, and I say, "Hey," back, but my voice is lost in the room of kids.
"You and I are on for tonight, right?" Lauren says. She's so pretty. Dressed up, like she's off for a job interview or something.

He shrugs. "Sure," he says, and he's glancing in my direction, but I look away before I can see if he sees me.

When Mrs. Pray starts teaching, I close my eyes and I think about Jesse walking into the room and in my mind it's me following, holding on to him, and setting up the date.

Taylor waits for me after English, another week gone. Like he did those few months before a weekend changed his mind. He's standing there in the hall, leaning on the lockers, waiting.

I stop so fast that someone runs into me and then gives me a shove, saying, "Jesus," at the same time. I stumble forward and Taylor steps to greet me. He says hello by lifting his chin and eyebrows, then he cuts through the crowded hallway and when I start walking away, he's there, walking in time with me.

"What?" I say. And I wonder where that Jesse is. "I thought," Taylor says, then he stops me by grabbing hold of my elbow. "I thought I could pick you up tonight. And we could do something."

His hair's combed forward and he smells good, clean. I can only watch his teeth when he speaks. They're white. He flosses, I know it.

I just look at his mouth and the whole time I'm thinking, *Kissing might help me*, but I don't say anything more and so he says, "Me and Heather. We're over."

I shrug. I know that. It didn't last even a month. It just

came at the wrong time, the leaving. I start walking again.
Jesse's in my head, so pretty, and Zach's there saying,
"Long skinny muscles can pack a punch."

"We had fun," Taylor says.
"You and Heather?" There are too many people in the
hall.
"You know I mean you and me."
I nod. "Sure we did," I say. "Until my brother died."
Someone slams his locker closed and I jump a little. It's
cold here in the hall, even with all these people.

Taylor's all quiet and then he says, "It's been a while now,"
all sad.
I stop moving, but Taylor walks a step or two farther.
Then he comes back and stands there in front of me.
He's not as tall as Jesse. And he's not dark-haired.
Something moves in my chest.

I think of Mom and Daddy and my brother gone and Jesse
who doesn't know me so what does it matter and Lauren
Hopkins and me alone, and I touch Taylor's lips with one
finger and his eyes close and I say, "Sure. Why not?"

The phone's ringing when I get home.

I answer it this time. Mom's car is gone anyway. Maybe she's with Daddy, helping him look through photos. Ha!

"Hello?"

"May I speak to London." It's a girl and I almost recognize her voice.

"This is she." I walk to my room, holding the house phone between my shoulder and cheek. Taylor will be here just in time for me to not eat dinner alone so I want to change my clothes.

"Well, this is Lili Fulton and I wanted to call and apologize if I hurt your feelings in the library. I didn't know about your brother. I just heard you were homeschooled and so were we for two years until my mother was ready to pull her hair out and ours, too, and I'm always saying stupid things. That's what my brothers say. But, London. I'm so, so sorry."

I take a deep breath for her. She didn't know about Zach? Maybe people aren't talking still. Someone said *something*, though, because NOW she knows. Whatever. And then I say it. "Whatever." It sounds really mean coming out of my mouth, but the word is there and I can't scoop it back up so I don't even try. WWJD?

43

What would Zach do?
WWZD?

"Do you forgive me, then?"

I choose a shirt from my closet. "Sure," I say. "Yes." My face has gone bloodred because of my rudeness. I can see it in the mirror on the door. I look away. "Sure, you're forgiven."

Lili lets out this little squeal. "Homeschoolers are the best. I know it's weird, but I've always been best friends with homeschoolers. You should come over. And we can talk. Or cook something great, but not anything like cinnamon rolls, because my mom still hasn't figured out the humidity. Can you?"

I slip off my jeans one handed and pull on leggings. They're black. Would Mom notice? And if she did, would she stop me from leaving the house? Would she actually *talk* to me? I check out my butt in the mirror. I avoid my face because this is me looking at my body in tight clothes in case a boy might want to see my butt too. The whole thing is sick.
The whole thing is not me.
Why am I doing it?

"I can't tonight."

"Then tomorrow?"

"Sure," I say again. And I don't let myself think anything about the answer because I'll cancel right then and there if I do.

"Tomorrow night," she says, and as Lili says something else, I hang up.

When Zach had sex the first time with Rachel, he told me three days later.
He said, "London, I can't believe it. I can't. She was so soft."

I screamed and covered my ears and he laughed, red-faced. Then he said,
"I love her, London." And I could tell he loved Rachel as much as Daddy loves Jesus, when he said those words.

I know what you're thinking. You're thinking what brother would tell his little sister he had sex? Mine would. Zach would.

You travel all over the world where there are just the two of you, and you become best friends.

Best friends.

Taylor picks me up as the sun dips away from the sky.
Daddy is still at his office.
Mom still hasn't come home.

When I walk outside, Taylor looks at me all green-eyed
and smiling. The color of the early evening sky reminds
me there is a God. It's just that beautiful. The color of a
crayon before you swipe it across paper.

There is a God. There is a God. There is a God.

I believe that. I do.

But does He believe in me?

"So what do you want to do?" Taylor asks.

He looks so warm and good I can hardly stand it.
I climb into the car, fasten my seat belt, and wait for
him to slide next to me in the driver's seat. It smells
like aftershave in here. I squeeze my eyes shut to the
memory.

"I like your hair."
I can't answer.

"You okay, London?"

I shake my head.

Taylor was my brother's best friend.
Not including me.
Not including Rachel.

Something is lodged in my throat. Aftershave maybe?

"Should we go back inside?" he says after a long minute.

I nod.

"Do you want me to go home?"

Yes. No. Yes. No. Yesnoyesnoyesnoyes.

I shrug.

"I can always come back."

"Okay." My voice isn't a whisper. It's less than that.

He's out of the car because now I can't move right.
He comes around the front, slouched over a bit, hands
shoved in his pockets.

What's wrong with me?
Who am I now?
How can one person leaving change you so much?

Taylor opens my door, unfastens my seat belt, takes my
hand. He almost has to make me walk. I wonder for a
second if I've forgotten how to live.

When we get up on the porch, Taylor puts his arms around
me. He pulls me so close I can feel the thread count of his
shirt on my cheekbone. "It'll get better," he says, then he
opens the front door for me, and I go back inside.

It will get better.
People always say that.
Like it really will.

I lean against the door, eyes closed, that aftershave smell
in my mouth.

Maybe he meant *we* will get better.
Me and him.

Not Mom and me.
Or just plain ol' me.
But Taylor and me.

Like Before.

Weekends kill me.
No pun intended.

They are sad. Lonely. Heartbreaking.
Three of us left and still we're all alone.

And what about this?
How did I end up responsible?
How?

I choose not to go to Lili's house, and when she calls I ignore her.

What if my mother started to care again right this
second?
Would I care if she cared?
Would I forgive her?

Yes.
Yesyesyesyesyesyesyesyesyes.

I'm weak and needy.
I need my mom.
I want my brother.
I don't have either.

We need each other to be whole.
How can one person take so much with him?

It is not fair.

Monday morning, when I walk outside for Daddy to
take me to school, I see Taylor. Fog sits close to the
ground and Taylor stands next to his car, right there in
front of my house, like Before. Like this is normal and
we've never stopped seeing each other. It's like my eyes
are going bad, the way he kind of fades from view a bit
as the fog thickens.

Daddy sees Taylor too, and I see Daddy pause, take a
step, pause, take a step, and then he walks right over
to Taylor and throws his arms around him. They're the
same height.

"How are you?" Daddy says, and Taylor says, "I'm okay.
Doing better." Daddy claps Taylor on the back and they
stand there a second and Taylor says, "I was going to take
London to school. If you want. If that's okay with you."
And Daddy says, "I'd love for you to. I've been so busy
down at the church," and Taylor nods and says, "We've
heard the first book is doing pretty well. My mom told
me to tell you we pray for your family every day." Then
Daddy nods too and says, "Thank you. London? Are you
okay with Taylor helping me out?"

I stand in the doorway, half in, half out, feeling like a
burden to my father, like the fog holds me back, books

tucked to my chest, the loneliness and safety of my house just a step behind me. "Okay." But, really, I'm not sure.

The grass is wet with dew and the tops of my shoes cool as I walk to the side of the road.
You can do this, I think.
I'm shaking.

What if the car has my brother's smell still? As I head toward Taylor, I know it does. Taylor and Zach were like brothers.

And when Taylor opens the car door for me, I smell I am right.

The drive's quiet.
Taylor taps the steering wheel, glancing at me every
once in a while.
I look forward, breathing through my mouth.

"Sorry about the aftershave," he says.
I sort of nod.
"It makes me feel better."

When I glance at Taylor, I see he's hurting too.
Zach's circle was a big one—it touched lots of people. I
know that with my brain, but my heart hasn't let me see
past me too far.
All of us are missing something, I realize as I sit there, the
Florida morning sweeping past my window. Like, lots of
people. Lots. Everyone knew Zach. Everyone loved him.

"How?" My voice feels unused and sounds that way too.
I don't look at Taylor.

The sun is bright. Cold. I can't wait for warmer weather.
Soon, right?

"It reminds me of him." Taylor taps at the steering wheel again. Pulls the car to a halt at the stop sign. "We bought this stuff together."

"I didn't know that."

I hear him swallow. "He told me you'd like it."

Now I do look at Taylor. The road to school is busy. We're only a few blocks away.

"I do like it," I say. "But it reminds me too much of him."

We look at each other. The space between us feels so huge. Someone beeps and Taylor, he doesn't move. Just sits there. Then reaches across the distance to touch my face with his fingertips.

He walks me to study hall. Drops me off at the door.
Waits for me to look him in the eyes. But I can't. I give
him a one-armed hug and feel his lips in my hair, feel one
hand on my hip bone.

"I don't need a ride home," I say. Then I hurry into class,
stumbling on a bit of sand, maybe, as I go through the
door.

No one talks to me.
They don't even look my way.
There's a death bubble around me and I know it. It's
a thin film, one that only I can see through, and I have
proof no one can see me, because they never look in
my direction
and I refuse to look in theirs.

As soon as I sit down, I wish I were with Taylor again,
riding to school or to the beach or to Tallahassee even,
my eyes closed, smelling my brother all around me.

It's that afternoon, in English class when Jesse walks past with Lauren on his arm, looking so fine I want to slug Lauren right in the face, it's that afternoon that I start talking to Zach.

Just in my head.
Maybe my lips move.
But no one talks to me.
Except maybe Lili if I would let her.
And Taylor, with his Zach smell.

"Zach? Zach? How are you? Are you there?"

He doesn't answer, and for a moment, sitting in that hard desk chair, watching Lauren kiss Jesse full on the mouth until Mrs. Pray tells her to stop or else, I miss my brother so much that I think I feel my heart is still split wide open.

I remember how Daddy said, "Jesus died of a broken heart."
And I think I know how that feels.

Right after he was gone, when we knew he was really gone, and we all stood with Zach as he died a second time, I thought I'd crawl right out of my skin with grief.

(Mom was done talking to me by then, had already screamed at me there in the hospital until a nurse asked her to quiet down.)

At home, I'd run to my room and cried out to Jesus. There would be no Lazarus miracle here. I knew that.

But
there was a pause in my grief
as I felt my brother edge his way into my room
like he had so many times before
and come up close to me.

I waited
quiet
afraid to move
like I might chase him away if I turned.

I could smell his aftershave, and I knew he was there to let me know he was okay.

That visit? It was real. I swear it.

But that visit wasn't enough.

I want more.
I want him back.
Why does death have to be so final?
I want to scream my question
pound at God's door
demand an answer
ask Him to forgive me
if I've done something wrong
and then give my brother another chance.

Taylor tries three times to take me home that
afternoon, but I cannot do it.

"I'll walk," I say.
"It's too far, London."
"Not really."

We're in the parking lot. Cars are everywhere. Driving
away. Beeping at one another. The cool air smells of
exhaust.
The noise makes me nervous, shaky. Maybe Mom's
silence has made me more sensitive.
Taylor puts his hand on my arm, and some kid leans out
a window and hollers, "Just say yes!"

I panic. Want to run. Want to get away. And so I do. I
rush right past Taylor, right in front of a car that almost
hits me.
"Stupid bitch!" The passenger screams the words, but
I don't stop moving until I'm stopped by the crowd of
students leaving C wing.

"London?" Taylor is close behind. I can hear him. He
grabs the sleeve of my jacket. "Please."

I see Lili then. She's coming out of the double doors just

down from where we are. She waves, her face breaking into a tentative smile.

I'd smile back if I could.

"She's taking me home," I tell Taylor. "I can't ride with you." I don't even look at him. I start toward Lili, whose smile grows a bit bigger, though she looks behind herself once.

Taylor grabs my arm. Turns me toward him. "What did I do, London? What?"

I feel a hand on my throat and realize with a start it's my own. I glance up at him. "You smell too much like my brother." Then I walk away, even when he says, "I can change that."

"That guy is hot," Lili says. "And he's still watching you."

I shrug. "I told him you'd take me home," I say. "Just nod like you agree."

"We can so do that," Lili says, sweeping her dark hair over her shoulder with one hand then giving Taylor a thumbs-up sign. "Where do you live?"

"You don't have to really," I say. Someone bumps into me, knocking the notebooks from my hands. I don't even have the energy to pick them up. I'm not even sure I can squat to gather these spilled things. I'm lucky that the crowd has thinned or I'd get trampled. Why am I so tired? All-the-time tired. Lili helps, grabs stuff up, hands it all to me. She's the only girl in the whole school dressed in summer clothes. What will she wear when it warms up around here? Nothing?

"Let's go." She's got on one big smile. Her face is so happy. I feel guilty about this, too, for ignoring her. How can she even forgive me when my mother can't?

"No, I just . . ."
"You just nothing," she says. "You just need a ride. Come with us."

67

I'm too tired to argue. And I need a ride. This once.
Next time I'll walk. Or ride with Taylor. Or maybe call my
mom. Ha!

We head down the sidewalk, passing Taylor, who
watches me, and to the sidewalk.

"Gosh, he's hot," Lili says, like it's an apology. We cross
the parking lot, to the far corner where an old van sits.

"The Beast," Lili says. And then, "Once we were at the mall
in Utah and we stopped in the parking lot and this old lady
climbed up inside our van like we were a bus or something."
Lili laughs, and I nod, because what else should I do?

She slides the side door open. "Gross!" she says, and
she's so disgusted I'm scared there must be some
monster in the back. "I'm telling Mom if you don't get
your mackdown sessions under control." Lili looks at me
and rolls her eyes. "We're taking London home."

So I'm all about clichéd crap, right? And yet I don't see
this coming. Jesse, moving from the backseat, wiping
lip gloss from his mouth. Lauren, coming up to the

front, Jesse letting her hang on to the back of his shirt, then grabbing her hand and helping her to sit in the passenger seat.

Of freaking course.

All the way to my house, Lili chatters.

I don't have to give directions, because Lauren knows
the way. We were friends for a long time. I liked her.
I really did. Lots of people do. Guys, too. She reaches
across the open space between her and Jesse, running
her hands through his hair every once in a while,
pointing the way to go, resting her hand on his thigh.

"Stop touching my brother in public," Lili says, and I can
tell she is *not* happy. "He may not care, but I do. And so
does my family."

She looks at me and mouths, "I can't stand that girl." I
almost smile.

The truth is, I still like Lauren. I would like her better if
she cared. But Lili doesn't need to know that.

"Your brother's a big boy," Lauren says. "We're just having
fun."
Jesse grins at Lili.

"I live here," I say as Lauren shouts, "Stop!"

The van screeches to a halt, and I open the door, taking

70

the huge step to the ground. My house seems lonely sitting there, like its insides have spilled out. Can everyone tell?

"Thanks." When I look up, Jesse stares at me and so does his sister. They're practically twins. I can see that they are related, though I have no idea how I didn't notice this before. "Thanks," I say again.

Lili leaps out of the van, hitting the ground with a thump in the gravel. "Now that I know where you live, we can hang out," she says. "We don't live so far from here. Want us to pick you up on the way to school in the morning?"

I don't say anything. Think how I should ride with Taylor because that's the right thing but know that I won't. Not now. Not right now.

"Taylor's back, isn't he?" Lauren says. "You know he dropped Heather." When I look at her, the sun seems to have picked her out and shines there, making her hair fiery. "She cried for days." No one says anything, and she speaks again. "That's what I heard."

I swallow. My skin tingles. "I'm not going with him. I mean, I did this morning, to save my dad the trip, but ..." My voice dwindles away.

"You back to talking?" Lauren says.
I just look at her, and she shrugs.

"Oh, that hot guy's named Taylor?" Lili says, and she breaks out in a smile brighter than the sunbeam Lauren sits in. "So we'll take you home *and* pick you up in the a.m. Is that good?" She turns to her brother. A cool breeze picks up and I can smell the ocean. "You okay with that, Jesse?"

"Sure." He looks me right in the eye, and all the sudden I want to kiss him. Is Lauren's lip gloss still on his lips? I want to find out. I almost take a step forward, there's that kind of draw. It's almost spiritual. Does he feel it too? He looks at me like he does. Then, without warning, Lili hugs me, and for a moment the places where her skin touches mine burn like ice.

"This is going to be so fun. We'll pick you up about seven tomorrow morning." She releases me.

I open my mouth to say okay but can only nod.

It's been a long time. My mouth, it only sometimes works.
I don't have that much to say
didn't have anything to say when it all happened
and now
with Lauren and Taylor and the others, maybe I'm used
to being silent.

But this Jesse, this Lili, they're new and they don't have
one bit of a clue what my life was.
What it is now.
So maybe I can start over a little on the inside.

I'm all alone.
When I step in the house, I feel the emptiness, feel me
the only person breathing in here.

For a moment I think of my mother being here every day
by herself
thinking of her dead son and the daughter she hates and
doesn't want to have anything to do with.

I walk into the foyer, which is dark as an artificial night, and
know I wouldn't want to sit around here either. I'd leave too.

There's a mirror by the front door. I force myself to look
at my reflection.

Am I so bad that my mother has to hate me?
Would I quit talking to me?
Was any of this my fault?
There's not one answer on my face, only sadness.

I have to look away.

I flip on the light and start through the house, turning on
switches and opening curtains and blinds.

The mother who hates me can close them all later. If she comes home.

She loved him best.
We all knew that.
I even heard Daddy telling her to love me better
and she just laughed—saying she loved us both,
but especially Zach.

I didn't blame her.
I loved him best too.

People who saw the three or four of us together knew.
It was obvious to everyone he was the favorite.
And sometimes my brother used that to his advantage.
But mostly he didn't. Because, except for a few small
little itty-bitty tiny things, my brother was all right.

It was Lauren. Of course. Lauren told Lili everything. At least what she knew, which I'm sure isn't accurate. That's how gossip is. Bits of truth sprinkled in with lots of crap.

And Jesse, too, I bet.
I bet he knows.
I bet she told him first.

They both know by now.

A weight settles on my shoulders. I can't even stand up under it.
I have to go to bed.
So I do.

In bed I wonder.

Does she tell Jesse that she wanted my brother bad?

Does she confess he never was that interested in her?

That once he found Rachel, he never looked back at Lauren?

Does she tell them that one time, when she spent the night with me, my dad caught her sneaking into Zach's room, late?

Does she tell them how we laughed together?

Does she tell them that she was an expert at teaching someone how to put on makeup?

Does she say that we were best friends. Best. Before?

Does she say how I called her after he died?

Does she whisper how neither of us could talk?

Does she tell them that Zach loved Rachel?

And that Rachel.

That Rachel was something else.

At first, I was like Lili. Jealous when Zach found Rachel. But he so totally fell for her, and she didn't mind sharing their time with me, too, so *I* totally fell for her. I mean, if you could have seen Zach with her.

My Taylor (he *was* my Taylor then) was like, "Okay. Wow. That girl is smoking, London."
I punched him a good one for that. "How'd your brother manage to catch her?"

Mom and Daddy hated that she didn't believe in the same God we did.

But Zach? He just grinned.
Took her hand at the table, kissed her once full on the mouth, right in front of Daddy, who looked away and would have crossed himself if he'd been Catholic.

Who could know everything then? Besides God?

Who?

Lying in bed all dressed and on top of the covers, I hear Mom come home. She's moving around, muttering, mad, closing the blinds. Closing the curtains. Snapping off lights too, I expect.

She has to know I'm here.
She has to know I'm the only one who would go against her wishes and let the light in.

Well, there's light when she drives, isn't there? Can she block the sun out, with her sunglasses?

She has to know I'm here. She has to see my book bag on the table. She has to know I'm in my room. Where else would I be?
I know she knows. I know it.
But she doesn't come looking. Just mutters and closes curtains and blinds.

How long would I be dead before she found me?

She's not coming in my room.
I know she's not going to look in here.
What's so different about today?
Light in the house?

Still, I wait for her. And when she doesn't come to tell me hello after twenty minutes, I turn away from the door and pretend to sleep for no one.

Here's what I remember best about Mom. My old mom. My Before mom.

Afternoon snacks when we came home from school. Dancing in the living room with my girlfriends and me. Teaching me the hard parts of speech, all that grammar I didn't think was important.

She would do anything for anyone. She turned the car around to give homeless people money. She combed lice out of little kids' hair. She helped mothers hang mosquito netting. She made people dinner when someone they loved died.

But when Zach died,
Mom didn't accept one meal,
not one visitor,
not even me.

She hasn't come in my room, not once, since my brother passed. Not even to peek in to see if I'm still breathing.

I check on her, though.

I only go to school because they make me. Mom is so done with homeschooling.

When Daddy comes home, late, late, Mom is already in bed.

I've gotten up. Done my homework. Made a sandwich. Watched a little TV. Talked to myself in the shower. Picked out what I'm wearing to school. Whispered words to Zach.

"You see how you left me? You see how you left me, big brother?"

My eyes burn, but I don't cry.

Some late-night show is on and I should have been in bed long ago, but I want to hear someone's real voice. The voice of someone who loves me (is there anyone?). Not just Jay Leno or Jimmy Fallon.

"Want some hot chocolate, Daddy?" I ask him as soon as he comes in the house.
I can see the tired all around his eyes.
I can see him looking for Mom but acting like he's not.
I can see that he's sadder than he was yesterday. There's pain in his voice.

Is he missing my brother a little more tonight?

Or my mother?

"Do you, Daddy?" I ask.
The room is dark around us, just a soft light that falls
from the family room, where I sat watching TV.

Daddy hesitates, then nods and says, "Yes, London. I love
it when you make me hot chocolate."

"We used to do that a lot together, remember?" I say
this as I head for the kitchen. I pull out milk and cream
and a Hershey's chocolate bar and vanilla and sugar.

Mom taught me this recipe, I think, warming the cream
and milk and breaking the chocolate bar into bits. I
remember me standing close by her side. Her letting
me use the whisk to stir the drink. Her laughing at my
brother as he tried to steal chocolate. All of us sitting
together. How old were we? How long ago was that? It
seems ages and ages.

I pile marshmallows into two cups.
I can hear my father speaking to Mom. His voice is low
and hers is soft, chocolaty. I almost stop moving. Will she
drink with us? I open the cabinet, just in case. Reach for
another cup. My fingers tremble.

"We about ready?" Daddy says. He stands in the doorway, alone.

"Yes," I say, and pour the thick hot chocolate into two matching cups.

I don't even dream.

Maybe I should drink hot chocolate more often.

Some days, like this morning, I walk to Zach's car (I have the keys now. Daddy gave them to me. But I'm afraid to drive. I'll do it soon. I'm sure I will.), where it's parked at the curb. With the morning sun just right, I can sort of see him in there. If I squint.

If I squint, I can see him, head tilted, laughing. Taylor's in the backseat, Rachel, in the front. I should be next to Taylor, but I have to close my eyes awful tight to see that.

When I get up close, there's dew that has settled all over the car. Someone has written MISS YOU in big block letters on the window. I can see a handprint on the hood, where the someone leaned, and streaks where the water ran.

For a moment I wonder if I did that. Did I sleepwalk out here and write those words? I'm pretty sure I didn't.

So who did?
Does it matter?
I close my eyes tight.

I feel this bit of calm, knowing that someone crept here in the night and that that person misses my brother too.

It's cold out here, and my robe and pj's aren't enough to

keep me warm. The sun is just waking, just breaking the horizon, slipping through the orange grove. I should have worn my slippers.

I clutch the keys. Imagine getting in Zach's car, even in my nightclothes, and maybe following my mother wherever it is she goes. I know I won't, but I like the thought of bravery. Maybe today will be a good day. Maybe someone new will talk to me. Maybe the person who wrote on Zach's car.

When I open my eyes, a bit of fog is moving in and the smell of trees gets caught in the back of my throat. Right near those words written for my brother.

When the van arrives, I run outside before Daddy
can ask me where Taylor is. A bit of me feels sick that
maybe he'll come here to pick me up. Will knock on the
door for me. I think this as I run through the grass. The
morning is cold, the sky still a bit gray.

Lili rolls down her window and says, "We have like eight
minutes before Queen Suck Face gets in the car."

"Oh," I say. "Okay." I heave open the back door, squeeze
in without opening it all the way.
Lili's been in the front, but she plops on the bench seat
next to where I sit down. My books are between us.
She's pulled her hair back with a hair band I bet her
mom wore. It's leather with tiny painted flowers.

"There," Lili says. "On to Queen Suck Face, driver." She
gives her brother a nod, and Jesse puts the van in gear.

"Lauren's not that bad," I say, but I'm not so sure who
she is now. I'm not sure who I am.

"See," Jesse says. "London says she's not so bad." He
glances at me in the rearview mirror.

I have to look away. He seems so different than . . . than

what? "I haven't really talked to her in a while though. Your sister might be right."

"No, you'll see," Lili says, settling the seat belt around herself. Over her shoulder, out the window, is the orange grove we were going to do something with. The leaves are so green this morning.

"She can't keep her lips or hands to herself. I expect her to pull his clothes off in study hall."

"Okaaay," Jesse says. From where I sit I see the side of his face go pink. For some reason, right at that moment, I think I fall in love with him. He's so beautiful and that shy thing is way appealing.

What? I am crazy. Have I gone crazy with all life and God have handed me? You can't fall in love, just like that, because some boy is gorgy and shy. My pulse quickens.

"She's . . ." I clear my throat and start again. "Lauren has always been like that. She's"—I pause—"physical."

Lili mumbles something not so nice under her breath, and I wonder if Zach would have spent more time with Lauren if Rachel hadn't found him.

Lili and Jesse go back and forth with each other, and
I only hear the sound of their voices, not their words.
Then this thought strikes me. If . . .

If Lauren had been his girlfriend, Zach might still be alive.

Zach? **I mouth,** staring out the window looking at
nothing. *Zach?*
Can you hear me?
Do you see me in this van?
Do you know I miss you?
Do you miss me?

By the time we get to school, I understand what Lili means.

Lauren *is* Queen Suck Face.

(Did she do that tongue thing with Zach? Why doesn't she care that we're in the van with her? Why does he kiss her back, stopping only when Lili hollers for them to?)

Lili gets out of the van in the school parking lot. When I climb out behind her, I can see she is madder than a hill of disturbed fire ants. Her face has two red splotches on the cheekbones and she grinds her teeth. Her hands are parked on her hips.

"Uh-oh," Lauren says, stepping to the ground in a pretty way. She adjusts her short skirt. "Little sister is mad." I know her well enough to see she's nervous. And Jesse must know Lili pretty well, because he's hurried to our side of the van.

"Keep your hands off my brother when I can and can't see you, Lauren." All around us cars are pulling into the parking lot. There's a smell of gas and cold and the sound of people getting ready to face a new day in school. Lili seems to hear none of it. "I mean it, Lauren. He's not going to have sex with you, and he's not going to marry you either. He has a girlfriend back home, and we won't be here in Florida forever. Jesse, you know that." She pokes him hard in the chest, and her backpack slides down to her elbow.

"I broke up with Shelly before we left," Jesse says. He looks at his sister, wearing a bit of a smile—an *I care* smile—and his eyes are dark brown. So dark I almost can't see the pupil. All the sudden he leans forward and puts his arms tight around his sister. "I won't do anything stupid," he says in this voice that melts me. Or is that the morning sun? Or a memory of Zach hugging me this same way? "We're just having fun."

Zach.
Oh, Zach.

I turn and hurry away.

They say time heals.
When?

It's been months now and I see my brother in
everything.

Instead of going to class, I hide in the library back in a corner where the school librarian caught Jason Easton smoking weed. I stay there, heart burning, wishing my brother would come back and hold me. Just one more time. That's all I'd need. Just one more.

Or—

I can almost not think it—

my mom.

I'd love a hug from my mother.

After a few bells ring, I make my way out of the library. Taylor will hug me. And I think I know what class he has, too.

The hall's empty.
The floor reflects the overhead lights, and as I pass
classroom doors, I can hear the buzz of students' voices
or teachers speaking.
It smells weird in here. Like dirty shoes or Fritos.

"Zach," I say. "It could be easier."
But is that true? I'm not so sure.

If my mother loved me still, would this horrible time in
my life be better?
I would still ache, right?
I would still miss him.
It would still feel as though part of me left when we
buried him, right?

And then I know: It would be easier. Because of Daddy.
He doesn't do it often, but if he just touches my
shoulder, I feel like I'm not alone.

Without meaning to, I'm running.
Just a touch.

I tap on the window. Faces turn toward me. But not Taylor. He's writing something from the board into his notebook.

The chair next to his is empty. Zach's chair. My brother's chair.
They retired his football jersey.
Did they retire his chair, too?
He's everywhere but here.
Wait, that doesn't make sense.

I tap on the glass again, and Mr. Crowe strides over and swings the door open. "Yes, London?" How does he know my name?

I'm mute.

Taylor glances up. His face changes when he sees me, and he's on his feet and walking to the door. No one says anything. Do they all know? They all must know. Everyone knows how it happened but me.
Wait, I know the how, not the why.
Wait again, I do know the why. . . .
I'm shaking.

Taylor brushes past Mr. Crowe.

"Hey," he says. His hair looks so blond.
"I miss him," I say before the door even closes behind
Mr. Crowe, who has left us here. "And there's no one to
tell."

"You can tell me."

He folds me close, pulls me right up to his chest. We
stand there and I want to cry. I want to cry but I can't.

Before,
when Zach was alive
and then gone

gone

I cried so long so hard so much that I couldn't breathe
through my nose and my eyes were almost swollen shut.

Now there is nothing for Zach
but my broken self
and not a thing to repair it.

In the car Taylor says, "Talk."
And so I do, while he drives.

I start when we were little:
how Zach would babysit me and squeeze my guts out
when he held me on his lap,
how he found me when I went to sleep in a closet and
everyone thought I was lost,
how once, when I was sick, he gave me his very favorite
Matchbox car (a big deal, seeing we were in Africa at the
time and hadn't brought that much from the States).

I tell everything I can think of.
My mouth dries out. My eyes sting. Taylor drives and drives.

"Remember what a bad surfer he was?"
"Remember how he couldn't sing at all?"
"Remember how he loved Rachel?"

The remembers go on until my head aches.

We drive along the beach. There aren't that many birds,
and the water looks like oil on the sand as it rolls up in
waves. Oil with bits of lace.

There are some things I don't say.

It's not *all* good.

No one is *all* good.

His unhappiness, I mean.

Taylor knows, Taylor knows, must remember, though he never says anything about it.

After the beach, Taylor and I drive to his house. No one's home.

I know where his room is and go there. Through the front room, down the hall on the left, past two doors (the bathroom, a closet).

I stand in the doorway. It's dark in here. The shade's pulled. A crayon width of light shows around the window covering.
(Has his mother caught something from my mom?)
Taylor snaps on the light.
His room is so neat.

Fully clothed, I climb into his bed, pulling the covers to my neck, turn my back on him, adjust his pillow under my head.

He's quiet.

On the wall nearest his bed is a picture of Zach on the football field, Taylor and a few of the other players gathered close. They won that game. I snapped the shot of the few of them, and Taylor printed it because, he said, "I can see a bit of your finger, London."
He was so corny.
Is he still?

After a moment he flips off the light and the room goes gray. I hear Taylor pad across the carpet. He pushes me over a bit, then lies on top of the blanket and wraps his arm around me. I can feel his breath in my hair. His knees are bent behind mine. He's pressed close. Does my hair stink?

"I miss him too," he says. He pulls in a big gulp of air and is quiet.

I jerk awake when Mrs. Curtis says, "Who the hell are you in bed with, Taylor?"

I feel him kick awake. He sits up, fast. "It's just . . . ," he says, and his voice is deeper than normal. "Mom? What are you doing here?" He gets up.

"I live here," she says. "And I'm home from work." She's mad.

For some reason I can't quite move. I've slept so hard I've drooled on Taylor's pillow. I smear my hand on the pillowcase, then try to flip it over.

"Is that you, London?"

"Yes." I try to get out from under the covers, but I'm stuck.

Mrs. Curtis is across the room in a few strides. She takes my face in her hands. Her palms are so cool I close my eyes. "Hey there, girlie," she says. "I've missed you." She untucks me, pulls me to my feet, and hugs me so close I think I can stand here forever in her arms.

When I get home that night, Daddy waits, arms crossed over his chest. He stands on the porch, right by the swing that I once flipped out the back of when Zach pushed me too high. I was fourteen. He laughed for hours over that. We hadn't been in New Smyrna but a few days.

Taylor takes my fingers in his hand. "We're still here, London," he says. "We've been trying to tell you so." He clears his throat. Looks at our hands. "I want to be with you."

"Heather?" I say. "What about Heather?"

He shakes his head. "No."

No. Okay, no.

"I lost so much," I say. It feels like the ghost of my brother crowds the front seat of the car. My father stands on the porch, waiting.

My father hasn't waited . . . "He hasn't waited for me in months."

Taylor says nothing.

"My mom, she doesn't really talk much anymore." I can't believe those words come out of my mouth. I'm embarrassed by them. The deal is, I want to say, "Doesn't talk much to *me* anymore," but my head won't let my mouth admit that fact.

Taylor brings my fingers to his lips. He talks over them.

"Just remember, I'm here, okay? I can keep waiting."

As I walk up to Daddy, I can see he's not waiting for me. Not really. Yes, he pats me on the back as I pass him, but he doesn't follow me into the house.

"You hear from your mom, London?"

I stop, my hand on the doorknob, backpack hanging from a shoulder. An almost warm breeze rushes past, ruffles my hair, moves on. Tonight's almost comfortable. And the sky threatens a late rain maybe. I glance back at my father, hoping he'll look me in the eye. Lightning splits the distant horizon. He stares away.

"What do you mean?" He knows she doesn't speak to me. I've heard him asking her to. I've heard her silence at his request.

"She hasn't come home today."

Okay. Okay then. "Where did she go?"

He doesn't answer, and I turn away. I'm numb inside. I'm ice. I'm raw. I'm cruel, unkind, alone, alone,

alone.

When the best part of a family dies, everyone falls apart.

I close the front door with a soft click.
How long will he stand out there?
Will he come in and check on me?
Will he remember I'm inside?

Where has she gone?
Did she go alone?
Does she miss us?

When I close my eyes here in the foyer, I see Mom's face
in the hospital.
She was so mad. So mad.
At me.
Like *I* had killed him.

And maybe I did.
Maybe I did.

In slow motion I make my way down the hall to Zach's room.
Mom hasn't changed a thing about it. It's exactly as it was.
The broken door hinges
splintered wood
marks on the white paint.

His clothes are on the floor. The covers on his bed are still messed up, like he left them that morning. You can almost see where he may have put his head on his pillow.

Here's the thing about life.
It twists away.
It feels right-perfect—and then it makes a wild turn worse than a roller coaster.

And how can anyone expect that?

I haven't seen Daddy in here. Not since a week or two after.
But I have seen Mom touching his bed.

It's so private, so mommy-ish, the way she touches where he'd slept, that I never let her know that I've seen

114

her do this. She'd see it as an intrusion. Maybe she'd
slap at me again. Maybe she'd scream her sorrow at me
again.

Instead, when I catch her
I am quiet
watchful.

I see her kneel sometimes, rest her head on his pillow,
spread her arms wide in the place he slept.
Sometimes her lips move, and I know she's talking to
him. You know, like I do. The whole thing, it's like she's
waiting for him to come back

home.

I want to say, "We're all waiting, Mom."
I want to shout it at her.
Shake her. Make her see
make her see me.

I want to say,
"No one wanted this."
"I miss him too."
"Look! at! me!"

But Mom is gone. Not just gone in the car, but gone
gone gone.

If anything like this ever happens to me again
anything
like
this

And I am the mom

And if there are other kids

I swear to God in Heaven that I will pull all who are left
close, and
never
let them
go.

I won't leave one out.

Lili calls right after I've finished my homework. It's like she somehow knows I've closed that last book, have just rested my forehead on the cover.

"London?" she says.

"Hey, Lili." My head's still down. The second L in CALCULUS is huge and blue. An ugly blue, at that.

"It's Friday night," she says.

"Yes."

"Are you going out with that really hot guy I saw you with the other afternoon?"
"No," I say. "Taylor and I aren't dating." I just slept in his bed all day, him so close I could feel his heart beat.

"Well, we do movies as a family on Friday nights. Want to come over?"

I swallow. Twice. "I'm not part of the family."
She laughs. She has a nice laugh. A laugh that means it.

"We can have *friends* over," she says. "We'll come get you. If you want. Will your mom let you?"

You mean the mom who hasn't wandered in yet? The mom I haven't had a conversation with in months? The mom who *hates* me? "She won't care." Truer words haven't been spoken in *this* house.

"You want to then? We're watching this old movie called *Blast from the Past*. Have you seen it? It's hilarious."

"Sure," I say, just like that, because now Daddy is gone, driving around looking for Mom, and the house is so quiet, so quiet, that I could stay here, yes, I could, or I could call Taylor or I could try to sleep but I am way awake and Lili has been trying so hard to be my friend and I still remember what is was like to be the new kid—twice at the same school. "Sure. Yes. I haven't seen the movie, but I'd like to."

"We'll be by in a few," she says. "See ya!"

Lauren isn't with them.

Lili drives, almost running into the deep ditch next to the road when she pulls up.

"In Utah we have curbs." She shouts out her brother's window and does that cute laugh.

"I've been praying she won't kill us," Jesse says.

"Praying doesn't keep people alive." The words are out of my mouth before I can stop them.

Jesse looks at me wide-eyed. Surprised.

If I knew how to chuckle, I would. Ease the discomfort.

He opens his car door, leaps out, and then opens the van door for me.

"Wow, thanks," I say. Even after my faithless comment, he's done something kind. Something my daddy used to do for my mom.

He takes my elbow. Holds me back. Lili watches from the driver's seat.

"Don't be sad, London," he whispers to me, then helps me into the van. He smells so good.

Don't be sad, London. I think it over and over. *Don't be sad.*

Lili's house is the opposite of mine.

Piled up with things, things all over, like people and voices
and toys and shoes taken off right here and just left.
This is sensory overload.

Mr. and Mrs. Fulton in the family room. Two more
boys—who look just like little Jesses—on the sofa. The
one in Pull-Ups can't be more than three. He stares at
me with eyes like dark chocolates. His bangs have been
cut too short.

"I'm sitting with you," he whispers. Then he stands and
takes my hand. Something slivery stabs at my heart.

I'm not sure what he's been eating, but it's still on his palm.
His mom and dad laugh like this is the funniest thing
they've seen all day.

"Nathan likes you," Mrs. Fulton says in a voice that
sounds just like Lili.
(Do I sound like my mother?)
Mr. Fulton gets out of his La-Z-Boy, shakes my free
hand—the wrong one—because Nathan holds tight to
the other. "He knows what he likes."
What can I say to that? *Okay?* I nod.

121

Mrs. Fulton says, "Natey, no. She's here to visit Lili."

The room is all overfilled with noise. Steve ("Hey guess what? I'm nine tomorrow!") walks across the sofa till he's right in the middle, then plops down.

"Mom," Lili says. She makes the word two syllables. I remember when I used to do that.

"They're okay," I say. "I like little kids."
"I'm not that little," Steve says.
"Right," I say.

Where is Jesse? I guess he's not watching the movie with us. My heart sinks.
Lili sits, pats the sofa next to her, and I ease myself down.
This family is too much.

This family is my family not that long ago.
This was my family, smaller, yes, but together.
Laughing. Snuggled close.

Alive.

The lights are out, the opening credits rolling, when
Jesse comes in with three bowls of popcorn, which he
hands out to his parents, Steve, and me. He picks Natey
up, then plops down close, settling his little brother in his
lap.

"Off the phone with Queen Suck Face?" Lili fake
whispers at him.
"I wasn't talking to her," Jesse says.
When I glance at him, he's looking at me. In the dark
he looks so familiar, so comfortable that I think maybe I
have known him all my life.

I sort of watch the movie.
But mostly I feel Jesse so close, and Lili right there, and
Steve and Natey and Mr. and Mrs. Fulton. Everyone
breathing. Everyone smashed together and warm.
It's like we are all on the sofa, all seven of us.
Squished side by side.

All the sudden the TV screen goes a little dark and no
one notices. No one but me.
"Hey," I say, and Jesse moves closer. His face near mine.
"What, London? Ya need something?"
Natey is asleep, his little hand loose in mine.
"The TV," I say. But I almost can't hear my words. There's
this buzzing in my ears, and I want to run, RUN!

Then Jesse does this weird thing.
He slips his arm around my shoulders, pulls me closer to
him.
I can hear his breathing, and I match mine to his.

"Queen Suck Face isn't going to like that," Lili says. On
the darkening screen Brendan Fraser dances.

"You all right, London?" Jesse asks.

But I've closed my eyes by now, and I'm just

concentrating on Jesse's breath going in and out until I'm okay.

"You better?" he says near the end of the movie. He moved his arm when my eyes cleared and I could see the movie again. How did he know?

I nod. "Yes. Yes." I nod again.

"I thought we were going to lose you."

Around us the whole room is quiet. Both boys are asleep. So's Mr. Fulton.

"I'm not sure what happened."

Mrs. Fulton moves on light feet, pulling the boys up, both at once, to tuck them into bed. "Don't go anywhere other than to and from London's home," she says to Lili and Jesse. Then she says, "I am so glad you're here, London. Really."

She means it. I can hear she means it.

"Can you spend the night?" Lili says. She's on her knees, looking at me. She has the best hair. "Would your parents let you? I have something you can sleep in. Some kind of jammies. We can talk all night."

How can she be so nice when I can hardly make a word come out of my mouth?

"Give her a chance to answer, Lili," Jesse says. He moves away and my arm, I notice, goes cold. "I gotta go call Queen Suck Face."

"Make me vomit, why don't you," Lili says. She rolls her eyes. "What do you say? Do you want to?"

"Sure." And I do. I take a deep breath and try to shake off this ever present feeling of grief. I can feel it dislodge a bit. Move some, from my shoulders.

"Oh, goodie!"
Goodie?
"Call your mom and see if it's okay."

I clear my throat. "I don't have to," I say. "She'll be all right with it."

We talk about:
* Boys at school
* Girls at school
* Queen Suck Face
* Utah
* Africa (and other family travels)
* How long ago we stopped traveling and settled down

Then, just like that, Lili is sound asleep.

"Lili?"
I'm on a pallet next to her bed. Her arm hangs down, creamy white, fingers relaxed. Her pretty face is almost hanging off the bed too, her mouth a little bit open.
"Lili?"

There's no sound from her but deep, slow breathing.

I lie on my back, look at the ceiling that seems clouded with the darkness.

Down the hall I can hear Jesse still talking to Queen Suck . . . I mean Lauren, my used-to-be best friend. I can't hear his words, and all the sudden I want to.

Should I?

Should I go listen in on him?

My heart pounds at the thought. I haven't done anything daring like this in so long. Well, not including sleeping all day with Taylor. But that doesn't count because it wasn't planned. My lips tingle.

I get up on my knees.

What's my body doing? I haven't decided to listen, and yet, here I am getting up like I've made a plan. Like *I'm* Lauren. How embarrassing!

But it's my body that's doing the decision making.

I crawl toward the door.

Look back at Lili, who sleeps on, her face like an angel's, in the dark room.

Outside the door, I stand up. Well, sort of stand up. I'm crouched over but I'm off my knees. My heart thumps. My mouth has gone dry. Do I have toothpaste on my lips? Why do I feel so giddy?

Jesse's voice is low and I can't make out the words still. In fact, I have no idea where he is.

Down the hall I go, crouched over like I have a spine problem. I cover my mouth with my hand. I'm grinning. Grinning.

There! He's there, behind this closed door. I can hear him, voice soft, deep from the late hour maybe? He speaks only a few words every now and then. A sigh from the bed. Maybe he's turning over. For some reason I think of French toast, me flipping it over on the greased skillet for Zach and him saying, "I could eat your French toast all day, London," and me saying back, "I'm not making it for you all day, Zacheus." I was mad that day. Why was I mad?

I don't hear anything about me, though I listen. I'm so dumb! Why would Jesse and Lauren talk about me? Ha! They've probably talked about sex. Or making out. Or how good-looking Jesse is.

It's quiet for a long moment, and I run my hand on the door. It's cool to the touch. Smooth. I imagine myself opening it, sliding into the room, sitting beside Jesse, kissing him right as he says Lauren's name.

Across the hall, one of the Fultons makes a sound. Are they getting up? And just like that, Jesse's door opens.

He looks startled, then he smiles down at me.

"What are you doing here, London?" He's so pretty it takes my breath away. Or maybe I'm having some kind of attack again. The truth is, I can't see him that well, because a light is on behind him. He's backlit. Glowy.

"I'm just. I. I can't," I say.
"You were listening."

I shake my head. "No. Not really." My face burns. "Lili's asleep and . . ."
He leans against the doorjamb. He's not wearing a shirt, and his chest looks so smooth I have the urge to run my hand across his skin, maybe rest my cheek on his . . .

"What are you looking at?"
"Huh? I'm not looking at . . ."

"I saw you."

Is he kidding? I think he's kidding. I try to smile, but my lips shake. "I better go back to bed." I fake a yawn. I turn, walk back, hands sweating, knowing, knowing that he watches me the whole way to his sister's room.

I dream about Jesus.

He's on a hill—a big hill—like a mountain or something. And just like that, there's Zach. My brother. The two of them stand together, and Jesus smiles like nothing else. Like He's so glad that Zach's with Him. It's like they're pals or something.

When I wake up, the sun is just starting to rise. I can see the morning at the window, peering in.

I lie still. I want to keep this feeling, this Zach feeling, this Jesus feeling, with me. Things seem so . . . I don't know . . . so right.

I go back to sleep before the sensation slips away, and I don't dream again.

"Morning, London," Jesse says when I walk into the dining room with Lili. He has this funny look on his face, like he's daring me to confess something. Confess my infatuation? I want to walk over and kiss him a good one, but instead I ignore him.

"You sleep good?"

"Did you sleep *well*," Mrs. Fulton says. "*Well*, Jesse. Did you, London?" She mutters to herself, "We have got to get a pull-out bed for guests."

"Sure," I say. I glance at Mrs. Fulton. Her back is to me as she pours huge bowls of Cap'n Crunch for her little boys. I stick my tongue out at Jesse. He just looks at me, waiting. But Natey sees what I do and gasps. He lets out a squeal of laughter along with, "London did something very naughty, Mommy. *Very* naughty."

"What's that, baby?" Lili says. She picks Natey up and tickles at him.

I have to look away.

"She sticked her tongue at Jesse," he says.

"Yeah, Mom," Jesse says, "London sticked her tongue out at me."

134

I'm horrified. "You're acting ugly," I somehow manage to say.

"Am I?"
I nod. I feel my face flame.
"How?"
I have no answer.
Lili watches us. "Keep flirting," she says. "You both know how I feel about Queen Suck Face."

There's this photo of me with Zach.
I'm newly born and he's just over a year old.
He's got me crunched up to his little self, and he laughs
as I kiss his face.
It's not a real kiss, of course, just a baby kiss.

I loved him from the moment I was born until the
moment he died.
I love him still.

I know I should go home. You don't spend the night with someone—last-minute invited—and *then* stay all day on Saturday. Moms don't like that.
Still, I have to make myself leave.

"I can walk," I tell Lili after breakfast as she hurries to get ready. She has a dance class that she's off to. Dance? Who does that? Normal people?
I am so not normal anymore.
Was I ever? I think so.

"Jesse will take you home after he drops me off," she says. She's brushing all that gorgy dark hair. She smiles at me in the mirror. "Do you like him?"

I'm holding this unicorn of hers. It's small, has a golden horn and tiny golden hooves. I don't expect her question. "Who?"

She sets the brush down, then takes me by the shoulders. Her room is a mismatch of colors that somehow work together.
"*You* know," she says. "*My* brother." Her voice is full of italics.

"Natey and Steve are just too young for me," I say. I can hear them in the other room. It's the first time I've made

a joke since Zach died. Wow. It feels good to say that
silly thing.
But it also feels like I'm betraying him. My brother gone
too soon.
My knees go a little weak, and I have to sit down on
the edge of her bed. The blankets from my pallet are all
folded. Resting.

"You know who I mean, silly," she says. She has a nice
smile.

I swallow. "I like him fine."
"Would you date him?" She still holds my shoulders,
even though I'm rag-doll sitting now.
I give a weak shrug. "He's not interested."

Lili turns back to the mirror, pulls her hair into a
loose ponytail. "I sure would like for him to be." She's
muttering. Bothered. "I do *not* like Queen Suck Face."

"Oh really?" Another joke.

Again Lili turns to me. She's dead serious. "She was *all*
over him that *very* first day we came to school. Like *all!*"

I nod because I'm not sure what to do or say. At last I get out the words, "He's pretty damn hot."

"Sure," Lili says, wrinkling her nose. "Sure he is." Then, "Ready?"

I nod.
I want to say, "I'd be all over him too." But I don't. I just follow her out the door.

Lili gives me this face/look when the three of us get in the van. It's like a wink without the wink.

"Take London home after you drop me off," she says. She pats my hands that I've folded in my lap.

"You are such a weirdo," Jesse says. He glances at us in the rearview mirror. "My little sister is weird," he says to me. Then he zooms off toward I-4.

Lili starts talking and doesn't stop until we've pulled into the Xtreme Dance Studio. A guy with auburn-colored hair leans against the wall, but when he sees our van, he puts this smile on his face. He saunters toward the parking lot and the stall where we pull in. And I'm not kidding about saunter. He really does.

"Oh great," Jesse says. "Little Lord Fauntleroy's waiting for you."

"Jeffrey's a gentleman," Lili says, and she looks at me and raises her eyebrows. "That's Jeffrey O'Rourke. He can really move. And he hasn't groped me even once though I want him to."

"I'll break his face if he gropes you," Jesse says, and I can tell he means it.

"I'm sure you will," Lili says. She pops out of the van, leans in the window. "I'm off to be groped." Then she skips over to Jeffrey, her dance bag swinging from her arm. He tucks his hands in his pockets and rocks back on his heels, smiling like all get-out.

"Right." Jesse throws the van in reverse. "I'll be back for you," he says to Lili, who turns, waves at me, calling, "See you later. Thanks for the sleepover. Love you, London!"

Love you, London!
Love you!

"Come up front," Jesse says.

I can't move. *Love you, London.*

He looks at me over his shoulder.

"Okay." And just like that, I can't get the image of him
shirtless out of my brain either. I don't look at his face as
I move forward, fasten my seat belt.

Love you, London.

We're quiet for a few miles.

I stare out the wide-open window, the wind blowing in.

I'm a little cold, and I roll it closed.

Don't look at him, I think.

Remember Taylor, so blond. So tender to me.

Think of Zach with Rachel.

They're so connected.

Zach and Taylor and Rachel. They're all together in my
head and heart. Almost one.

ZachTaylorRachel

and me

with them.

And this Jesse.
With Jesse, there are no memories.
He's free and clear
except for Lauren.

Jesse says, "What are you thinking, London?"

Outside, the morning tries to get warm. The sun's so
bright I squint.

"Nothing," I say.

"Not thinking about me?"

I can't find my tongue for a moment. When I do, I
stumble over it. "Lauren's my friend. I mean, she used to
be my friend." I glance at him.

His grin is wicked. "She doesn't own me," he says.
We pull up in front of my house.
In one glance I see that Mom's home. There's her car
and Daddy's, too.

Jesse parks the van. Turns off the engine. He unbuckles
his seat belt and then unbuckles mine.
With his fingertips, he turns my face to his.

His hand cups my chin, and he kisses me. Nothing big deal, that kiss. Except it *is* a big deal. His lips taste like syrup, but I know he didn't have pancakes for breakfast. He didn't have waffles, either. He ate Cap'n Crunch with his brothers.

His fingers leave burn marks on my cheek.

"I've been wanting to do that since English class that first day."

"Oh," I say. I can't look him in the eye. If I look him in the eye, I might kiss him again. No, I *will* kiss him again. "Well, thank you." Somehow, I open the van door and stumble out onto the green, green grass of our lawn.

I am the stupidest girl at Smyrna High.
I am.

Daddy is in the kitchen.

Has he watched me from the window? He stands at the sink, coffee cup in hand, eyebrows knit together.

I try to glide past, but I'm on shaky feet.

"You know what Jesus says about fornication," he says.

"Excuse me?" I slow.

"You know what He says."

"Ummm." Coming in from outside makes the house seem darker than usual. Why hasn't he opened the curtains? He knows they've been closed for months. Or maybe there's something wrong with my eyes.

"You didn't come home last night."

I look him straight in the face—no problem looking at *him*—and say nothing. What does he care, huh? What. Does. He. Care?

"First your brother and now you," he says.

My daddy knows I promised to wait to have sex. To wait until I'm married.

"I can't watch you do the same things he did. Destroying our family. Destroying himself."
Here's my voice. I find it now. "Don't you dare say anything about Zach." I clench my hands into fists. "Don't you dare."

I find my feet, too. I turn around and go right back outside.

His lips were so soft.
Love you, Lili.

I just walk.
There's no place to go, really.

But when I get to the cemetery, I know I've been out a long, long time. We live a good ways from the cemetery.

Zach's burial site is on the east side, because Daddy wanted him closest to Jesus when He comes again. "He'll come from the east," Daddy has said. Is that Scripture too? Like fornicating?

Daddy's written about both and preached that to the little congregations everywhere we traveled. But that's not what he said in Africa or South America or Mexico. There he said, "Charity never faileth."

I walk to the farthest, most eastern part of this plot of ground. The sky looks like it's been covered in marshmallow fluff, there are that many clouds. Every once in a while one creeps over the sun, and for a moment I feel colder.

Then there it is. His tombstone.

ZACHEUS LEE CASTLE
GONE TOO SOON
DEAREST SON AND BROTHER

I lie on the ground, right where I think his casket might be. I wish I could put my arms into the earth, put my arms around Zach, just one last time. The grass isn't soft, but tough, strong, Florida grass.

"Dear Jesus, dear Jesus." This is a sincere prayer. "Please let my brother hear me."

I tell Zach everything. It's a repeat, these words, a cry of loneliness.
How I miss him.
How I'm starting to feel alive again, but only a little bit alive. Sort of zombie-ish.
How I'm scared to death (no pun intended) to do this alone.
Without him.
This wasn't part of my plan.
Part of his? Maybe.
But not mine.

"Why did you have to go so early, Zach?"

I wait for an answer. Sometimes—and this is the God's honest truth—sometimes I know he's near. If only for a moment. But not this time.

A bit of breeze moves past, and even though my eyes are closed, I imagine that the grass is bowing before that wind.
Maybe bowing to Zach.
My brother.

Once, when I was little, really little,
something awful happened.

We were in South America, the whole family. And Zach
and I, we couldn't have been more than four and five. We
lived in this village, helping to dig wells, when this sickness
went through and everyone died. Like, I mean, *everyone*.

I still remember.

I remember Daddy came into the place we were staying
and said, "We've got to go. Now."

We left.
Everyone else stayed.
And died.
Including a little girl and her twin sister that I was friends
with. Those two had thick, thick brown hair. Always
braided. And tiny white Chiclet teeth. I remember.

Afterward I heard Daddy talking to Mom.
Heard Daddy telling some officials.
And Zachy got sick.
Oh, how Mom worried over him.

We left and got shots and took antibiotics and Zach got better, but no one else lived, including those two little girls I played with every day,
those little girls with the brown hair and
Chiclet teeth.

That night, after all that dying,
after hearing what had happened,
I lay in a real bed
with a light sheet and a real pillow.

Facedown.
Crying.
And this is true.
Swear.

Jesus touched me.

I felt His hand rest right on my back,
between my shoulder blades,
and I felt so much better
because I knew those little girls were with Him.

I just knew it.
With a touch.

I only told Zach about that.
And he believed me.
Believed in me.
Like always.

We were like those twins, Zach and me. As close.
He was my hero, my best friend. Always believing, always
talking, always there.

Zacheus.

Unlike my mother now.
Unlike my father.
My Zach always believed in me.

Here's the thing about Jesus's broken heart.
How much did it hurt?

Sometimes
Sometimes, I'm sure I know.

Somehow, I can't believe it, I fall asleep on Zach's grave. And I dream.

In this dream Mom's there. And it's my old mom. She's smiling, so that's how I know it's the old her. "I love you, London," she says. I hear her voice. See her reach to pet me. Her hand never connects to my face, though I wait for her touch. Stand there. Wait.

I wake up, roll onto my back, still waiting for that touch from my mom. The marshmallow clouds have gone dark. Stormy.
It can't be that late, can it? Where's the sun?

I'm hungry.

"And lucky," I say to Zach, "that fire ants didn't find me here and eat me up."

"You okay?"

I scream, sit, go dizzy.

It's the groundskeeper. An older guy, dark hair going gray.

"Sorry," he says. He keeps his distance. "I knew you were alive. Saw that you were breathing. You see everything out here. You okay?"

I nod. "I think so." I clear my throat. "I'll go."

"Stay as long as you like," he says. "You're safe here."
He gets into an old blue truck that probably used to be the color of the sky.
Drives off with a tilt of his head to me.

He might be an angel. I don't know. He might.

I have a few dollars in my pocket, but I quit my cell phone a long time ago. Just let it die in my bedside table drawer. I couldn't face all the text messages, the calls, the are-you-okays?

(No! No, I wasn't okay! Got it? I WAS NOT OKAY.)

My angel's "You okay?" is different.
I close my eyes.
Am I getting a little better? Healing a little? Aching less?

I stand, look back at the grass to see if there is a print of my body
(there is),
and walk on out of the cemetery, checking all the while for the groundskeeper, who I don't see again.

So, not too far away is a 7-Eleven.
In the bathroom I see I have grass-mark dents all over
one side of my face. My mascara's smeared. Did I cry
in my sleep? I have cried while sleeping plenty of times.
Awakened with tears streaming down my face.

I use a paper towel and brush at my teeth. I would try
the soap but decide against it because it's bar soap and
someone has left black scum on what used to be a
white bar.

"Don't be ridikerus." I can almost hear Zach say the
words. He always said that. "Don't be ridikerus. You don't
brush your teeth with soap, no matter how your mouth
tastes, London."
Does he say ridikerus still?
Does Zach say it to God? To Jesus? To someone else but
not me anymore?

I leave the bathroom, which I can all the sudden
really smell, and walk into the store. There are a
few customers, including a grandma-type lady who
shepherds around two little kids, a boy and a girl, who
ask in tiny voices for this treat or that.

I've not eaten all day and I realize I'm hungry. Outside,

the sky turns darker and the wind picks up. The clouds race away from the beach. A bit of salt smell from the ocean tries to sweep away the odor of strong coffee and hot dogs when someone opens the door, but the food smells win out.

So I buy an all-beef Big Bite Hot Dog. Just looking at the crinkly thing on the rolling grill makes my mouth water, and after I pop the wiener into a bun, I load on the ketchup, mayonnaise, and relish. I get a fountain Coke, too, adding lots and lots of vanilla, making sure I save some change, because I don't want to walk all the way home. Gonna have to call someone for a ride. I've walked so far I feel like I need a hip replacement.

When I step outside, a gust of wind blows garbage across the parking lot. I am so hungry, I'm shaking. But I take small bites of the Big Bite. Enjoy every bit. Sit there on the corner of the sidewalk and eat the best hot dog I have ever tasted. Sip at the vanilla-y Coke. Then, when I'm licking my fingers, I breathe deep through my nose, closing my eyes, wonder who to call.

Daddy?
Mom?
Zach? (Ha! Another joke. One that makes my stomach clench. Makes the all-beef Big Bite Hot Dog lurch.)

I think about Lili and Jesse.
And then there's Lauren.

But I can only seem to remember Taylor's number. So that's who I call.

"Come get me?" I say. I stand at the phone booth missing its phone book.

"Yes," Taylor says, even though I can hear he's doing something else, can hear a bunch of people talking. Someone laughs.

"You can wait, if you want." A horn behind me blares, kids (no, they're older than I am, a car full of guys) pretending that I'm in their way. Or something. "If you want, you can come later. After your thing."

"I don't want to come later. You home?"

I tell him where I am. Pretend to not see the guys (four of them).

"Okay." He doesn't say good-bye.

I hang up the phone. Turn.

"You need a ride?" one guy says.

I shake my head.

"Sure?"

"Sure."

The wind blows drops of rain onto the sidewalk, and everything, just like that, smells dirty and hot, though the wind is cold and I wish for a jacket.

Then the rain seems to disappear, and even though the storm is heavy in the air around me, I sit still, crossing my arms. I can wait.

I will wait.

And if it starts to rain, why, I'll hop back inside and see who's gracing the cover of the *Enquirer*.

I wait awhile before I start walking home.
Against the traffic so I can see Taylor's Toyota.
The weather's holding, so why not? And, anyway, it seems
to be taking Taylor a long time to get here. Was he at a
party? With another girl?

Maybe I should have called Jesse.
I should have.
But I don't know his number. Can't remember Lili's. Or
my mother? What about my mother?
That thought sits in my stomach with the all-beef Big
Bite Hot Dog like a joke. It's cold, the idea of my mom
not wanting me anymore.
Did she ever?
I walk, head down, the unhappy breeze pushing me along.

The rain is hesitant now. There were those few drops
at the 7-Eleven, a few every once in a while, and then
there's that car of guys. They drive past, circle around,
pull in front of me. Did they wait for me?
There's no sidewalk, and I feel my heart start to pick up.

It's not dark. The sun still has a way to go to dusk even.
Still, everything is so gray out here. Maybe my eyes are
failing. I think grief makes your eyes stop working as

well. For sure, colors aren't as bright and the sun isn't as warm and . . .

"We'll take you home," one guy says. He has a nice smile. He sticks his arm out the window, reaching for me, as I hurry past the Cadillac-size car.

Without meaning to, I hunch over a little farther, then stop and straighten, because doesn't hunching mean I'm scared?
And I'm not scared. Not really. He has a nice smile.

"Help me, Jesus," I say.
The sky opens up then.
I'm past the car full of guys.
Hurrying.
The rain comes down fast. Hard. So hard it hurts, stings.
"Well, thanks for that."

"Come on!" More than one of them call.
"Someone's coming for me," I say.
I feel like I'm in a bad commercial. The rain commercial, and when I get home someone will hand me some hot tea and my hair will spring into perfect curls.
"You're getting wet," Nice Smile says.

"Sure am."

They don't get out of the car. The rain has saved me. The
talker just hangs his tanned arm from the window. They
back up like I pull them along on a rope. Rain water
starts to puddle. That's a Florida storm for you.

Taylor drives up then. How did he see me in the rain?
His car lights are on.
All the cars' lights are on.
When did it get so dark?
How did I not notice?

Taylor gets out of the Toyota, walks like he's going
somewhere important, taking big steps, right up to me.
Then he pulls me in to his body, and I feel the dryness of
his clothes.
He just holds me. Tight.
I work my hands out of my pockets and to his waist.
Grip the material of his shirt.

"You're getting me wet," he says into my hair.
His voice is so different from Nice Smile's.

"I'm sorry." I say this into his shoulder.

There's rain in my eyelashes. I think it's rain.

He pulls in a breath. "You remind me so much of your crazy brother."

The car of guys must leave, but I don't hear them. I just stand in the rain with Taylor not that far from where my dead brother is buried and remember how Zach loved the rain.

After Rachel moved,
after Zachy died,
I tried to get ahold of Rachel maybe a thousand times.
But she never called back.

She loves the rain too.

Once, the four of us picnicked on the beach.

We watched as the sky grew dark out over the ocean,
watched as the storm drew closer,
then closer, watched as the rain pelted the sand almost
like bullets.

I sat there on a blanket, arms around my knees, Taylor
so close I was warm down one side. He rested his head
on my shoulder, and every once in a while he kissed my
face and muttered sweet words. After a bit—we were
already wet—he held a second blanket over us, to shield
us from the stinging rain.

Closer to the surf
Rachel and Zach ran at the waves
and away,
laughing like maniacs.

Taylor said, right after I thought it, he said,
"They're crazy together, London. Did you ever think he'd
find someone as crazy as he is?"
"I never did," I said.

Taylor looked at me then. He pressed his lips to my
forehead. "I love you, London Castle," he said. His breath

173

was warm, and I felt crazy happy myself.

In fact, I felt
right then
that everything in our world would have a happy ending.

"**What are you** doing out here?" Taylor asks. We're in the car, and I'm dripping all over everything. My hair has turned to ringlets.

I look at him side-eyed. "You know."

"Yes, but why alone?"

When I open my mouth, the words are trapped, and I have to cough to dislodge them. "There's . . ." Can I tell him? Can I say, *The whole family is gone? We've disappeared with Zach? Been buried with my brother?*

I shake my head.

Without warning, Taylor pulls the car over to the side of the road. There's a ditch next to us, filled with fast-running water.

"Look at me, London." His voice is stern but not angry.

Was I staring at my hands? I think so. I turn my gaze to Taylor.

"I'm here." He taps his chest. "I'm here. I'm always going to be here."

He shakes his head. "You said we needed a break. I didn't want a break. *You* said."

I nod. I asked for that when things started to crumble. When the yelling started. Before it was all over.

"I don't want to go anywhere," Taylor says. "Didn't want to."

"You're not even eighteen." Those familiar words are in my head, loud. And I say them to Taylor.

He looks out the window, which has gone all steamy. "I know what I know. I know how I feel."

I wasn't allowed in for The Talk.

Zacheus wanted me there. Wanted Rachel. But Daddy and Mom said no—like they already knew where this was headed.

And then the words came.

"I'm a religious writer! A missionary! You're the son of a religious writer. Of a missionary! You're not even seventeen!"

"So what! So what! What does age matter? I love her."

"You're too young to love anyone."

Mom's words were like a slap to Zach. He told me so, later.

"How will you take care of three people? You're not even out of high school." Mom's voice was razors. I could hear that myself where I stood hidden in the hall. And then after a thousand beats, "What will the neighbors think?"

"Where are we going?" Taylor asks.
We creep along, that's how hard the rain comes down.
We're blind.
"Your house?"

I don't say anything. I'm exhausted. Limp from almost-living. From trying to live in a place that is crooked, where I can't get a grip on anything.

"Mine?" he says.
"Yours."

"My mom's not home."

Mine is, I want to say, but that's a lie. Bodies that don't speak aren't a presence. They don't count.

Zach on the hospital bed.
Slight bruises on his neck.
His lips tinged blue.
Hooked up to everything.
Already looking gone.

Is he gone?

How can I stand it? How? My legs won't hold me up, and
I fall, catching myself at the foot of his bed.
Across from me, Daddy has given up praying that Zach
will make it. It's three days later.
My brother's an organ donor. "We can't let the organs
fail," the doctor says.
"Right." That's my father's voice. It comes from a tin can.
It comes from a different world.
Right?
And Mom, screaming at me as the time comes to let
him go, screaming at me!

We are a family, lost.

I've never told anyone about all of it.
Not about all of it.
Not Zach talking to me before.
Or him telling me about the baby.
(Or the fight. Oh! The fight!)
Or how my lungs felt so crushed inside that I couldn't
let any more than a gasp of air between my lips

when it was finished.

"Do you remember the first time we met?"

I sit on a bar stool in Taylor's kitchen. The storm rages on outside. I have on a pair of his shorts and a giant T-shirt of his. Even his socks are too big for me, the heel hitting up above my ankle.
I shake my head.
He slices two BLTs in half, puts them on creamy yellow plates.

"What? The girl *always* remembers. It's the guy who doesn't."
I offer him a bit of a smile. "I can't keep a lot in my head. Sorry."

Taylor pads over to the fridge, pulls out a big bottle of Coke, and pours two glasses full. "Want ice?" he asks as the Coke reaches the tippy-top of the second glass.

"No, thanks," I say.

He brings the drinks over, sets one in front of me, then slides the sandwich over too. He settles on the other bar stool. Lightning changes the colors of the kitchen to an odd white-blue, then thunder rocks that whole house. The lights go out. We're in the dark.

(I'd still be walking if Taylor hadn't picked me up. Would Mom care if I was struck dead by lightning coming home from my brother's grave? Or hit by a car? Or picked up by a bunch of rapists? Would she care?)

"We were over, a bunch of the football team, for hamburgers. Remember? Your dad was cooking them."
"What?"
"When we met. The first time. And you got that weird round brush caught in your hair, and your mom thought it would have to be cut out. But your dad and Zach got it free and burned a whole grill of burgers."

Lightning splits the sky again, and it sounds like the thunder might be right on top of us this time.

I cover my ears. Close my eyes. "You were there?"
Taylor laughs. "Yes. I was the guy drooling all over myself. I thought you were so pretty, London."
More lightning. More thunder. And me saying, "Oh!"

Sometimes I cannot swallow for the pain.
Even here, with Taylor, where I know I'm safe.

Sometimes I feel like I'm still stuck in those last few days.
That I can't get past anything that happened.

That the last real moment for me was hearing my
brother, Zach, alive.
I keep trying to remember him that way.
Remembering his last day with me, his room, dark. Him
so sad.

But there.
Right there where I could reach out and touch him.

Sometimes there is no air or too much air,
there is no floor,
no real feelings,
no truth—
not even from my father.
My daddy.
The missionary who writes about God and goodness.

It's like God shook the world side to side, and for some reason I can't find my feet under me.

Taylor and I kiss for a long time, even though I said I had to brush my teeth (his mom has a year's supply of toothbrushes in the bathroom closet), even though I said his mom wouldn't like it, even though I thought of Jesse's fingers burning on my face.

His mouth is minty, Colgate minty. His breath hot. My hands are in his hair, on his neck. When I pull back from Taylor to take in air, I see the lights have come back on. "London," he says. His eyes are closed.

Mrs. Curtis's opening the front door then. I hear the key in the lock. Hear the door open.

I put my hands on Taylor's face, one on each side. He opens his eyes. He takes my wrists in a gentle grasp.

I press my lips to his again. A good-bye kiss that feels like fire. Stand. Dizzy. He runs his hand up my leg, just under the bottom of those too-long shorts. When was the last time I shaved? I worry about it a second, then decide I don't even care.

"Oh, London," Mrs. Curtis says, surprise in her voice. She looks right away worried.

"I'm going home now," I say, though I don't want to. Nothing waits for me at my house.
I feel dead there.

"Where are your clothes, honey?"
"She got caught in the storm, Mom." Taylor stands up behind me, slips his arms around my waist, rests his chin on my shoulder. He's never done anything like this in front of his mom before, even though we dated for months. "They're in the dryer."

Mrs. Curtis gives a little nod.

I want her to touch me so much, I miss a mom so much, I miss my mom so much, that I break loose of Taylor's hug and walk to her. I kiss her face and her cheek cools my lips.

"Thank you," I say. "Thank you."

Do the dead feel pain? Do they? Is Zach still hurting?
Still fighting?

Is he as sorry as I am?
Burning in hell?
Is there purgatory?
Is there a prison for him on the other side?
Does he stand in a room full of devils?

I won't believe it.
Not for one awful mistake.
Not when he was loved so much.
Not when he loved so much.
I refuse to believe any of that.

Taylor takes me home, the whole way holding my hand.
The rain has stopped. Has darkened our world.
"I'll get you for school on Monday, okay?" He says this
without looking at me, just staring at the road ahead.
Our headlights cut through the steamy darkness. Trees
crowd us from the sides.

Jesse and Lili go through my mind. "I have a ride
home though," I say. "But I'd like it if you got me in the
mornings."

My mind says—or is it Zach whispering in my brain from
the dead?—*Start your day with one. End it with the other.
Tsk, tsk, London.*

Taylor looks at me. Did he hear Zach? Did he?
Shhh, I think. I *would* like it if he picked me up—if I saw
him first thing.

"Okay," he says.

We're quiet all the way to my house. There's no moon.

And then we see someone.
Ahead on the road.

Someone—I can see them now, though we've
slowed way down—someone in my brother's hoodie,
his number thirty on the back. New Smyrna High
Barracudas. The colors red and black.

I choke.
"Zach?" I say. Though I know this can't be. Something is
wrong. Not just that my brother is dead. Something else.
"Zach?" My voice is a whisper.
"London, no," Taylor says. "That person is too small to be
Zach." But his voice sounds weird. He's not sure either.

At once I want to jump out of the moving vehicle, run
to the person ahead of us. I also want to get away, drive
in the opposite direction. A scream rises in my throat,
and I stop it with my hand. Just hold my neck. Hold it till
we pass.

She looks me right in the eye as we go by her.
My mother.

"Don't stop," I say as Taylor slows the car. "Don't."
"But . . ."

"Please." My heart jumps in my chest. I squeeze Taylor's
hand in both of mine. "She's out walking." The lie is there
for the taking. "She does it a lot."

To tell the truth, I don't know *what* my mother does
when she leaves the house anymore.
"She needs to be alone."
I don't know this, either.
But
I cannot bear the thought of my mother ignoring me as
we try to give her a ride. I can't hardly think it now.
I saw the look on her face when she recognized me.
I saw it.

I don't let Taylor open my door.
He hasn't even turned off the ignition and I have my
foot out, ready to go.

I jump out of the car and run, holding my clothes in
one hand—keeping Taylor's shorts pulled up with the
other—to the front door. The porch light is on and I
run to that. I hear the car whine as it backs up. I splash
through a puddle. Every step I take, every one, builds a
rage inside me.

When I reach the porch, I slip on the wet wood, almost
falling. Then I throw the door open so hard that it
bounces on the wall.

"Hey, hey, hey," Daddy says, appearing from the back of
the house. Then, "Oh," when he sees me.
Like he doesn't know I live here.
Like he's surprised I showed up.
Has he forgotten me already?
I was only gone one night in all these months.
Once!
And then this day. This day when he didn't check on me.
This day when I was gone after a night away.

My mouth opens. The words come out. I don't even
know what they are till I hear them in the air around us.

"*I* didn't leave forever."
Daddy pauses. His face goes slack, like our separateness
was holding it up.

"I know that, honey," Daddy says after a few seconds. He
reaches for me, but he doesn't try that hard, and when
his hand misses mine, he just lets it dangle at his side.
"But she doesn't," I whisper.
"It's hard for her, London."
I tilt my head. Look at him more closely. Does he know
what he just said? Did that really come out of his mouth?
"It's hard for all of us. All of us."

"She was his *mother*, London. You'll understand when
you're a mother yourself."
"She's my mother too," I say, so worn out my mouth
might never work again.
Then I head to bed.

If Zachy's death should be hard on anyone, it's me.
Yes! All of us! I admit, all of us. Everyone who knew him.
I'd never take anyone's sadness and keep it as my own. I
can hardly hold what I carry now.
But his going is hard on me.

Me!

I hear her come in later. Much later.
I hear the low mumble of my father's voice.
I hear her speaking, trying to keep calm. Trying to keep
her voice low.
There's silence for a bit. Then my father's voice. The door
to their bedroom opens and closes.

I wait for my mom. Wait for her to come talk to me.
I'm lying in bed, all my muscles so tense that I wonder if
I'll get a headache.
I'll forgive her for ignoring me.
I will. She doesn't even have to apologize.
If she comes in. Just steps in and says my name, she's forgiven.

She could even yell and I'd take her back.
She could yell for me leaving her on the roadside.
She could yell for me opening the blinds.

I don't care.

I hear footsteps in the hall.
I hear breathing. It's Mom, right?
I hear her light step move past my room, past my open
door, past me, and on down the hall to Zach's room.

I used to be alive too. Really alive.
We all did.

Thump thump thump thump thump.
Thump thump thump thump thump.

Thump thump thump.

Thump thump thump.

Thump thump.

Thump.

Thump.

Nothing.
Nothing.
Nothing.

I wake from my own screaming.
Heart pounding.
Hands sweating.

"Zach!"

Daddy's at my door before I can make my eyes open.
I'm crying.
Shaking.
Afraid.
Poisoned from the nightmare.

"You okay?" he says.

I nod.
Find my voice. "Yes."
Let my eyes open just a bit.

Daddy stands there, one step away from being in my
room. His hand rests on the wall, and he leans toward
me. Doesn't walk inside. "Well, all right then."

I'm cold like snow.
I need him to hug me, but he doesn't walk into the room.
Just stands there. Leaning. And lets me thaw on my own.

I lie back down. Tuck myself in. Wrap my own arms
around me in a hug from me.

When I look back toward my bedroom doorway, I see
my daddy's gone.
Without a word.

And I know then, I know, he blames me too.

At school the whole world pretends I'm not there.
They look away when I'm near.
Walk around me like I'm a stone in a stream and they're
the water.

I've gotten pretty good at pretending too.
I only cry sometimes. Always in the bathroom.
I sit in the back of the classroom.
I look away.

But Jesse and Lili have changed this complete aloneness
for me.
They smile, though Jesse doesn't approach when he's
with Lauren. Just clasps her hand, lifts his chin to me.
Lili runs up, chattering like she hasn't seen me in weeks
instead of two classes.

And Taylor, he walks like he stands at the edge of a
cloud, waiting for the fog to clear so he can get up close.

Today,
though, something in me changes. Was it my dream?
My mother in my brother's football hoodie? Daddy not
quite coming into my room?

I feel the change as I dress.
Like I'm cracking apart.
As I eat breakfast alone.
Stretching in an uncomfortable way.
As I walk past my mom, who doesn't even look up
from her novel and coffee, the overhead light flicked on
instead of the shades lifted and the curtains opened.

When I call Lili to say I have a ride, I feel sick to my
stomach. What's wrong with me? How can I even feel
what I'm feeling? I wait outside in the morning sun, dew
sparkling on the grass, and I feel the change and worry
over it, like I'm working at a loose tooth.

("I can pull that out," Zach said, more than once. "We
can share the money Mom gives you."
He pulled out three of my baby teeth, both of us
working at them, before Mom found out what was going
on.
She laughed.

Can you believe it? Laughed! And said, "Zacheus, your sister needs her teeth to eat.")

I haven't been outside long before Taylor drives up. I grab my stuff. Hurry to the car, to him, throw the Toyota door open. Do I look as different as I feel?

"Ready?" he says, and I'm across the emergency brake, hand on his thigh, mouth on his mouth. He kisses me back, touching my arm, the car rolling forward until he puts the gear in park. My hands are on his face, pulling him close and closer.

He looks at me when I pull away.

"Good morning," I say, and he gives me a raised eyebrow look.
"Hey."

That feeling? That change? It's there still. Heavy.

I put my hand on Taylor's face. "School?" I say.
"Not so sure anymore," he says, but he shifts the car and drives us to class.

"I'm trying to get into choir," Lili says when I see her in
the hall. "What do you think, London?"
She's in my space and it's strange—comforting.
Like medicine for my illness. I want to hug her. Hear her
tell me she loves me. Does she really?

Jesse glances at us over his shoulder as he stops at his
locker. Sends me a smile.
Is he thinking of that kiss? Our kiss?
I am, and my face burns at the remembrance. Especially
with Taylor at my side. Does he know? Can he read the
look Jesse gives me? Am I making it up?
How does my new skin fit? Is it too tight or too loose?

"I think you should try out." I say this having no idea if
she can sing or not.
Does it even matter with our choir?
Can I even remember *listening* to our choir?
I think I was just the sister of the best tight end the
'Cudas had seen in several years.

I was a football sister. Not a choir listener.

Now who am I? An only child changing in the
hallway at school.

More changes.
They are so different
so different, the two of them.

How can I be interested in two people like this?

Because they are the same, too, in a simple way. In a
tender, simple way.

I feel the change as I walk into the building.
Feel the change at my locker.
As I grab the right books for my morning class.
As I watch Taylor walk away to his class.
As I see Jesse and Lauren together.
See Heather in the hall with another guy (who is that?).

Jesse's in my head. All in my mind. Taking over.
I can't push him out, or away, from my thoughts.

My insides shift too.
I feel . . .
Not so alien.
Still alone, yes, but not really, because I have three friends
and they may not know everything but they know enough.
And they don't care. Or maybe it's that they *do* care.

My stomach is full of electricity. And sometimes I can't
quite see because of the jittery feeling. I sit through
study hall and do nothing but shade a whole piece of
paper gray with my mechanical pencil.

In calc I pretend to listen. But I can't keep my mind on
Ms. Stephan's explanations.

I only think of kissing.

Of hands and tongues and things that would make my
mother melt if she knew what was in my brain.
And I'm thinking it about two guys.
Two.
I can't even look at Ms. Stephan.

I am far worse than my dead brother.
Zacheus doesn't hold a candle to me.

What would it be like to kiss them together
both at once?
To have them touch me
at the same time?
I am so sick.

Sick!

But I want to see Jesse
Now
and I don't know why the thoughts are here
Now
don't know what I have done
Now.

In the movies, I'd snap the pencil I hold in my hands
not tremble the way I do.

My thoughts are in control.

As a man thinketh ... I can hear Daddy's voice.
Oh yeah?
What about this, I'm a girl.
As a girl thinketh?

The metamorphosis rages by the time I am out of my seat and into the hall between classes.

It takes over my feet. Makes me move toward Jesse when I see him alone after second period. He's in the hall. I've sought him out, gone looking for him, something I would never do Before. I'm going to be late to class.

I see him through the crowd, see his look of surprise when he sees me, that slow smile of his.
Whoever I'm becoming makes me grab his hand when I get close to him and pull him away from his locker.

"What?" he says, letting out a bit of a laugh, trying to close his locker door before we get too far away, me dragging him along. "What is it, London?"
But I am too surprised to answer.
His eyes are dark, dark. And his face is so pretty. It looks like he didn't shave today.

Someone laughs as they hurry past us, and I pull him into a doorway, the classroom behind us unlit.
"What are you doing, London Castle?" Jesse says. He smiles, but his smile seems worried. Or his face. His face seems worried. Or nervous. Yes, nervous. And that's sexy too.

212

I want to say, "I'm not sure, Jesse Fulton," but instead I put my arms around his neck. I have to stand on tiptoe. He's thinner than Taylor, and he smells like clean laundry. Does he wash his own clothes? Or does his mom? I rest my head on his chest, breathing deep, pressing close to him, hoping this acting on the metamorphosis means I will feel better inside.

For a second he stands there. Hesitant. Then he puts his arms around me. Just holds me. Just holds me. And when I kiss him, a long kiss, comparing his taste to Taylor's, my hands gripping his shirt, he kisses me back.

The bell rings.
"Get a room," someone says, and someone else says, "Get some for me," but they're background noise that doesn't matter.

My face is hot, my heart pounds.

"We're going to be late," Jesse says. He sounds breathless. Or off balance. The way I feel.

"Right," I say, then turn and leave him standing there, and head to class.

I've become a kissing addict. I think that's it. The buzzy feeling. Burning lips. The foggy eyes. Maybe I could kiss every good-looking guy here at school. Maybe even the good-looking male teachers. The thought warms me and troubles me at the same time.

"That was weird," Jesse says when I get into the van. We have only a moment together, and I want to run my hand over his face, but I sit down as though nothing has happened between us. I settle my short skirt around me like a fan. It's the best purple color ever. Dark pinkish purple.

I give Jesse a bit of a look. Lili climbs up next to me and plops down with a sigh.

Then Lauren is in the car. I give *her* a sweet smile. An I-know-what-your-boyfriend-tastes-like smile.

"You didn't wait," she says to Jesse, and he looks at her, eyebrows raised, then glances at me. Her voice is a pout. Her whole face bugs me, but I look down at my skirt, think how pretty it is. Think how it's the color of a butterfly and how I'm like a butterfly too, with all this evolving I'm doing.

"Why'd you look at her that way?" Lauren says.

"At who?" Jesse says.

No one says anything, then Lili speaks. "You have an active imagination, Suck Face."

Am I a Suck Face?

Maybe. Maybe I am.

Gosh, I hope so.

Do I want to be? Yes, maybe I do.

"I *imagined* my boyfriend not meeting me at my locker?"
She's mad. I don't look to see. Now I stare at the
window, keep my face straight, pet my skirt.

Jesse starts the van, and I stare out at the parking lot
full of cars and students, look for Taylor's old Toyota,
think about my brother driving me to school, wish I had
the nerve to kiss Jesse again and claim that name for
myself. "Queen Suck Face." Or something bigger. More
powerful—like "Oprah Suck Face."

That works for me.

I don't want to go home. I don't. The closer we get to my place, the more my muscles tense up. Going home means maybe a stop to my mutation. I can't even hear anyone's words, just the sounds of their voices. I want to be here. Stay here. Stay where my friend tells me she loves me. Where I'm maybe "Oprah Suck Face." Where two good-looking guys see me and want to be with me.

The sun rests in the sky at a slant.

"We're here," Lauren says. "London, get out."
"Shut up, Queenie," Lili says. She turns to me, her face bright. "I'll call you, okay?"
"Okay," I say, and when I get out of the van, I notice my skirt's not as bright as it was.
I watch the van drive off. See Lili waving out the back window. I stand there.

Where to go?

I start walking. Leave my backpack hanging from the mailbox and move. The afternoon is cooling off. I'm glad for my short jacket but sorry for the short skirt. My legs are cold.

"Zach? Have you been watching over me? Have you seen me?"

What would he think?

Would he slap hands with me for this or tell me to treat his best friend better?

I stop in the middle of the dirt road. Close my eyes. I know what he'd say.

But, this is all his fault. Zach's. If he wasn't dead, I'd be making wedding plans with Taylor maybe. Or college plans.

I keep trudging along until I find myself in our orange grove—maybe right in the middle—where all the air smells tangy and the trees are tall enough to block the setting sun.

"Zach," I say. I don't feel him close, like I want to. "Don't be mad at me, 'kay?"

There's nothing but the sound of a mockingbird. The wind cools. The sky is blue. Clear.

I sit down, away from sandspurs, feel the sand beneath me, look at the raggedy trees.

I've grown raggedy like that. But at this moment, in
this place, because of the change, I feel okay. The kisses
behind me. The kisses that may wait for me. I like this.

"Maybe it was that kiss," I say to Zach. And, "Maybe I
could live out here until summer's good and strong and
then winter sets in again. Maybe. Mom would never
notice if I left."

And then this weird thing happens, and all at once I'm
thinking about Rachel Bybee. It's like I hear her voice,
or see her picture, she's that clear in my mind. For a
moment I am stuck sitting there in the orange grove.

"Go."

I hear that word. I do.
And the next thing I know, I'm up, on my feet, walking—
then running—then out of there and down our sandy
lane to home.

I call her three times.
Her old cell phone number.
Over and over and over again.

But she doesn't answer. Just says, "This is Rachel's number. Leave a message if you want me to call you back."

I don't. Leave a message, I mean. Maybe I will soon. The next time I call.

Rachel broke up with Zach.
It was a teary separation.
No.
It was worse than teary.
It was horrible. Her parents waited for her in the car,
engine running, tapping at the horn every minute or so
for her to hurry on up.

Daddy and Mom stood behind Zach, arms crossed. I
watched out through the screen door, hands clenched,
teeth clenched. Crying with my brother and with Rachel
Bybee when her father came and dragged her away.

That's true.
Zach held on to her and then her daddy was there and
my mom, and Daddy did nothing but look away as my
brother ran after his girlfriend. (She didn't want to go.)

I ran out on the porch, hoping I could change things, but
I couldn't. I couldn't change anything. And Mom, she told
me to shut up.
She said, "London, you shut the hell up. It's better this
way."

Then the Bybees drove away. All the way up north.
And Rachel called two days later to say she wouldn't

see Zach again. That she understood her momma and daddy's feelings now and she had her own life to think of and that she was way too young to have a baby. Way too young.

And Zach, he died.
Killed himself three weeks later.

And it was me who found him first, Mom one step behind.

He was depressed.
You know how depressed he sometimes got.

Not always, but it happened,
the sadness, like after that little village died
or when he saw mangled bodies on the side of the road
in another country
or he watched something awful on TV.

Those kinds of things just wiped him out.

Daddy stopped his ministry abroad.
Daddy tried to pray his son better.
Daddy insisted Mom not homeschool us anymore.
But Zachy, he got sadder and sadder.

We came back for him. Here, to the United States, so
he'd be safer.

Mom tried to hug it all away.
Tried to do things, special mom-and-son kinds of things.
Tried to cook it better. Read it better.
We didn't know then how it would end up, or maybe
we would have made lots of different changes earlier.

Like admitting we needed help.

Someone should have made him get up after Rachel left
should have stayed with him
should have known it was going to happen.

They should have known.

I should have.

I *should* have.

This is what I sometimes think when I'm alone. This is
sometimes my prayer. My prayer for forgiveness from a
brother who left me behind because I didn't get it.

After he died,
after she heard,
Rachel Bybee called.
She had a new number. I didn't answer and she left a
message on my voice mail.
She was crying. Hard.

"I just found out," she said. "I miss him so bad, London. I
want to talk about him. Please. Call me and tell me what
happened. My heart is breaking."

By then my heart was already broken, so I never called her
back.
I let my phone run out of battery and I wouldn't have
picked it up even if my cell always worked—not if there
was a chance she could reach me. She was a part of this
whole thing, right?

I lost count of the number of times she called.

I feel bad about that now. Not taking her calls. But I
blamed her, too.

Tonight, after I phone Rachel again (no answer), I decide to start dinner.

I can cook. I can cook stuff from all over the world. I can eat spices that would blow out someone else's stomach. And I do, too. But tonight, Mom sitting in the living room, I decide to make something else. Not too hot. Something she'll like. Beef Stroganoff. She missed that most when we were overseas. I'll make that.

(Maybe she'll eat with us. If Daddy gets home in time. And she isn't as unhappy or mad or as whatever it is she's been. Maybe *she's* feeling a change too. Has she kissed two people?
Someone other than Daddy?
No! Of course not.)

We don't have any of the ingredients, so I decide to head over to Publix.

I work to keep my head clear when I get into Zach's car. He tried to teach me to drive, because Mom didn't have the patience and Daddy was too busy. As soon as I adjust the seat from his last drive (how long has that been now?), I hear his voice.

"London, just ease the clutch up when you're ready to go. That way you won't give us whiplash." I always gave us whiplash, and it's no different now. I smile at the memory, at how I feel sort of *good* in this car. Holding on to the steering wheel he held on to, sitting in the seat where he sat, pressing my foot to the same pedals.

There's this bit of him in the car—I'm not sure what—but I'm surprised that I have avoided sitting in here, driving, so many times.

The sky looks the same as it always does this time of night: clouds building over the ocean, moving this way fast. The sun is shiny as a dime. When I get into Publix, I run in and think, *Yes, tonight shopping* is *a pleasure.*

I like my skirt again. A boy in produce stares at me, nods when I look his way, and I kind of recognize him from school. *Should I kiss him?* I think, and grin at the silliness. I nod back, grab things I need, piling everything in my basket.

It's weird what's happening. The more I shop, the happier I feel. By the time I get to the car, I'm ready to slay the dragon—I forgot that's what Daddy used to say about Satan and instead of following Satan we should slay him by doing what's right. My heart feels bubbly, and I decide—just like that—I'm inviting Taylor over.

I drive past his house and his car's not there. I sit parked near the mailbox, but he doesn't come home. The sun's sinking fast, so I start back to my house, and when I get to the first stop sign, Taylor comes wheeling around the corner, music so loud I can hear it. He glances at Zach's car, recognizes me (I can tell by the look on his face), screeches to a halt, turns around, and pulls up next to my window.

"London," he says. He seems happy to see me. "What are you doing here?"
"I came by to ask you to dinner."
Another car tries to squeeze past us.
"Wanna come over? I'm cooking." I lift the bag I put in the passenger seat. It's heavy.
"You kidding me? I sure do."
"I'll drive," I say, and pat the wheel.

Taylor goes to speak to his mom, and I try four times to put the car in reverse and settle on just turning the thing around and going back to his place. I don't park in the driveway. The wind blows. The sky is the color of a blue flower plate with a rim of gold-orange closest to the earth. It's so beautiful I think, *I've slain the dragon.*

Maybe I need to spend more time in this car. Or cook.

Or pick up Taylor. Or kiss Jesse in doorways. Or try
to reach Rachel. Or sit in orange groves. Something.
Because I feel terrific. Or as close to terrific as I can
under the circumstances. We're less than a year out.
Nine months out and I'm driving and I feel pretty good.

Taylor comes outside, jogs across the front lawn. He's changed his shirt. I bet he even brushed his teeth. I can't help but smile.

Would Jesse do those things? Or just get into the car with me? Just drive away.

"Hey," Taylor says when he closes the door. His aftershave is different. Not so sweet as before. Not so Zach, and for a minute I feel this weight of sadness in my heart.

But I've slain the dragon and done so many wonderful things today that I'm going to swallow the grief and pretend it didn't happen. He puts the grocery bag on the floor between his feet. Mrs. Curtis watches from the door, waving.

"I like your mom," I say, pulling away from the house. I beep a good-bye to her. "She's nice."
Taylor nods.

"She's okay." His voice is teasing. He reaches over, puts his hand on the back of my neck, smoothes his fingers

through my hair. For a moment I can only see in black
and white. "She needs me to take her to see her mom
in St. Augustine tomorrow. Think I can trade rides with
Lili and they get you in the morning?"

"Sure." I nod. I drive to the end of the street, where a
whole thick row of hibiscus bushes leads up to the stop
sign. "I called Rachel," I say, just like that. What's wrong with
my mouth? It betrays me by kissing everyone and speaking
words I don't even know are there. Is it part of the
metamorphosis? Now the evening colors are *too* bright.

"You're kidding." Taylor looks at me, and I almost drive
off the road looking back. When did his eyes get so blue?
Does he need a haircut? I bet I could cut his hair. I used to
trim Zach's. I was supposed to trim his the day before he
died, but the fight started and Zach wouldn't let me turn
on the light and then, when it was too late, and when I
asked Mom to let me trim his hair, she wouldn't.

I wanted to do that for my dead brother. Trim his hair.

"What'd she say?" Taylor's hand is gentle.
For a moment I'm thinking he means Mom, but then I
realize he's talking about Rachel.
"Nothing. She wasn't there."

232

"Did you leave a message?"

I shake my head. I haven't left a message any time I've called. "I'll try her again. I need to." Wrong. I *have to*. I know this like I know I'm holding on to the steering wheel. I need her to understand that Zach loved her and he would have been a good father and even with everything that happened he would have forgiven her.

I'm not sure about that. Not really. But I'll tell her that anyway.

The thought of an abortion makes the fading light outside dim a moment.

("Her parents don't want her to have the baby. They want her to get rid of it. She's going to . . . she's going to . . . ," Zach said. "They want her to, because she's so young. And I could hear her mom and dad telling her to get off the phone." His room was dark dark dark. He hadn't showered in days. "That baby," he had said. "My tiny baby." And I cried myself to sleep that night.)

Taylor and I pull up to my house. When we get out of the car, the sun is gone. "Let's go cook," I say, taking his hand. "You can help."

This house is empty.

I make arrangements for a morning ride with Lili and Jesse and Queen Suck Face, then set the table for the four of us, and Taylor talks about a couple of colleges he wants to go to, maybe, and asks if I've thought of going anywhere, but I haven't and I shake my head and fold napkins, pale pink, pink as sweet baby lips. I set out candles, dim the dining room lights. Place quartered lemons on the glasses' rims for later.

In the kitchen, Taylor slices the sirloin and I get everything else out of the bag. We're quiet, working side by side. So close that his forearm touches mine sometimes, and I'm sorry right then that Zach couldn't get married, and didn't live, and that he saw so much sad stuff when we were little and that he won't have sex again or kiss someone he loves or let me trim his hair or slice the sirloin.

But I won't think of this tonight, because if I do, I'll fall and I have to keep away from the edge of the hole I am always standing near or falling in or trying to climb out of. I'm different, right?

How can my mood change so fast?
Why must I think at all?
I don't need to.
I swear I won't.

When everything is simmering, I push my way
between Taylor and the sink, where he's washing—no,
scrubbing—his hands. I put my arms around his waist,
rest my head on his chest, hear his heart beating on its
own—with no help from anything—and I want to cry
but I'm not going to. Instead, I tug air into my lungs—
lungs that work on their own—and force myself to
smile. It seems to help.

"Let me dry my hands, London," Taylor says, the words in
my hair. But I don't move.
"It must be this house that's killing me," I say into his shirt.
He puts his fingertips on my hip bones. I can feel the
cool dampness bleed through to my skin.

When I move away from this hug, I see the clock. It's six
thirty. I put the brown-and-serve rolls in the oven and
my heart pounds, waiting for my parents. "Will you let
me cut your hair, Taylor?" I ask. "After dinner?"

"Sure," he says, not even hesitating.

We eat, just me and Taylor, watching *America's Funniest Videos*. Mom hates it when I consume anything anywhere other than the dining room or kitchen, but I do it tonight because why the hell not? We end dinner with a root-beer float and me carrying a fat feeling of resentment.

I want to say it. I want to say, *She could have come. They could have come.* But it's so obvious that it's embarrassing. Of *course* my mom and dad should be home for dinner.

When Daddy comes in, he finds the two of us, on the couch, dishes piled on the coffee table, Taylor's arm around my shoulders.

I snuggle closer when I see my father, hoping Mom will be behind him. She isn't.

"It's nice to see you, Mr. Castle," Taylor says, then he clears his throat, and his fingers tighten on my shoulder. He says, "London waited dinner for you." He clears his throat again. "She waited an hour."

I move away and look at him. He's looking over his shoulder at Daddy, and Daddy hasn't even had a chance to say hello, but guess what? Taylor's right. I rest my hand on his arm. His skin is so warm I want to kiss the place

236

where I touch him, but that might seem weird, what with my daddy standing right there and all.

It takes a moment for Daddy to get his feet under himself. "London." He speaks like he didn't hear Taylor, and that embarrasses me. "You know I don't like it when you have friends over who are the opposite sex." And I say, "I know, Daddy. But we wanted to surprise you by making dinner. Plus, I'm cutting Taylor's hair for him soon."

Do you remember, I want to say, *that I cut Zachy's hair?*

"I'm not so sure that's a good idea," Daddy says. "Your mother won't like it."

"My mother's never here. She doesn't give a damn what I do."

Wait.
Who said that?
The room is so quiet it seems even the host of *America's Funniest Videos* takes a breather to hear what was said.

And then I know. I did it! I said it!
The words are out.

They're out—yes, in front of somebody—but they're out, and I feel so good to have said them I can't sit still. "She's not here now." I hold my hands out for him to see.

Daddy waits, his own hands just hanging there, and I think of Jesus and the cross and the nails the Romans pounded into His palms, and I take Taylor's hand in mine and say, "Let's go trim your hair."

Once, a long time ago, when we were in Haiti, when I first started cutting Zach's hair, I chopped a huge hunk out of the back. And when he saw it in a handheld mirror, he laughed and threatened to cut my hair too, but instead brushed it and braided it and patted my head.

For good measure, I think.

Taylor's hair is so soft, so fine, and there's so much of it that when I'm done trimming, it's all over my bathroom sink and floor. He looks at me in the mirror. He's sitting on my desk chair that we dragged into the small room, staring at me.

"What?" I say.

"I shouldn't have said that to your father, London," Taylor says. His face turns a slow pink. "He's a good guy and all. And I only meant . . ."

I stand behind him, the scissors in one hand, an orange comb in the other. He dips his head, and I can see his neck. He doesn't have the huge football player neck— and it's not too skinny, either. For a second I see a rope around it, and I drop the comb. It makes a sharp sound on the tile. I bend over to pick the comb up, my hands shaking.

"I only meant, I can see you're sad all the time, London. And I know you have reason to be." Taylor looks at me in the reflection. His eyes have gone glassy. Is he going to cry? "I'm sad too. He was my best friend. Not my brother. But I can't stand that your dad and mom didn't show up tonight."

He doesn't cry. I turn off the light, sit on his lap, and let him hold me in the darkness, my ankles curled around his.

I take Taylor home, walk him to the front door. There's a light on and we stand on the front porch and I kiss him good night.
I drive away, conking out the car only once, on a hill. Mom's still not home.

I clean the kitchen, go to bed, say my prayers on my knees, covered by the sheet and lightweight blanket.

I say the things I usually say to God: "Why? Why? Why? Let my father see me again. Let my mother care. Please don't let it hurt so much." But I notice something. Where the pain is? I feel a little hope, too.

I'm almost asleep when I hear my father in my doorway. "Good night, London," he says, his voice low, like he knows I'm asleep and there's some unwritten rule that he'd better not break. "I love you."

I love you.

"And I'm sorry."

I open my eyes. "Daddy?"
But he's gone, and to tell the truth, I'm not sure if he was a dream or not.

In this dream I stand with Jesse.
His hair is long, past his shoulders, and when he looks at me, I can't look him in the face.
When he kisses me, I feel so good inside, I think I'm healed.

All that time with Taylor and I dream of Jesse.

In the morning, even before I open my eyes, I can't wait to get to school.
I want to see Jesse.

And I want to see Taylor.

And I want to see Lili.

I throw back the covers, hurry to the bathroom, and shower.
The water's hot, and I'm so grateful for hot showers every time I take one, because believe you me, I know what it's like to bathe in cold water and even what it's like to take sponge baths, which are okay if the weather is warm. I suds up my hair, grateful for sweet-smelling soap, grateful for the new day and a tub.

Am I a freak? As I wash my body, I think, *It's supposed to be a year when people start to feel better and it hasn't been a year but I think I'm feeling okay.* A tentative okay feeling. I smile into the shower spray. Even with Mom being crazy—I'm used to that—I'm okay this morning.

As I step out onto the bath mat and dry off, I decide that *nothing* is going to ruin the day for me.

Mom sits at the dining room table sipping coffee. She's dressed up nice, but she doesn't raise her eyes to me when I set my books down. How can she be so perfect in her ignoring me?

Something tough runs down my spine—makes me stand taller. I think, *To hell with this, because nothing is going to ruin my happy-ish feeling. And I am sick of her game.* I think that, over and over, as I go into the kitchen, pour myself bran cereal, and make myself toast. Then I do something I haven't done since before I quit begging her to talk to me. I take my food into the dining room and sit down in the chair next to hers. I'm so close I can smell her perfume.

"I missed you at dinner," I say, and take a big bite of cereal. I'm shaking, and I think the bran is going to get caught in my throat and then maybe I will die too, like my brother, but it turns out I can swallow. Maybe all this bran and stress will just end up as diarrhea.

Mom proves she can swallow too. Keeps swallowing her coffee. Holds her cup in both hands. She looks off across the table, away from me. I can hear Daddy in the bathroom. Just up, I bet. Lately I am to school before he leaves for work, but I'm not so sure my mother ever sleeps.

"It was pretty good," I say. "Stroganoff. Your favorite."
Nothing. Not even a slurp in my direction.
She won't ruin this almost good beginning of a day. I won't let her. Anger wants to bubble up, but I push it down.
"I'm thinking of maybe making curry tonight. Another one of your favorites."
Still nothing.
"Unless you want something else. I could make hamburgers." My hands tremble, and my eyes fill with tears. I fight to keep my voice steady. In the other room the shower goes on.

Mom picks up her saucer and walks away, into the kitchen. I hear her put the dishes in the sink. She has to walk past me again to get out of the house. I'm glad. She hesitates. I can hear her waiting.

So she knows I'm alive. She knows!

I keep talking. "Or a pizza. I can go with Taylor, you remember him. I can go with him to the store and get

248

what we need for that. Fresh basil and mozzarella." My
feet have gotten me up and walked me to the doorway,
like they have a mind of their own. My mother stands at
the sink. Looking into it. She's so thin. But she's dressed
to perfection and her hair is done and . . . "What do you
think of that?"

When she walks past, she shoves me aside, hard. But I
pretend like that hasn't happened. And that weird mouth
of mine takes over.

"I'm here and you know it."

Mom goes to her room, grabs a sweater from her bed.
Goes to her nightstand and gets her purse.
Outside I hear the horn beep. It's Taylor, come to get me,
the Living Girl. Mom slips off her house shoes and goes
to her closet.

I feel so much pain watching her that I can't hold it in.
Tears stream down my face. The horn sounds again.

"I have two boyfriends," my mouth says. I wipe at my
cheeks.
Her shoes are on. She shoves past me a second time.

She's touched me! Twice!

"Neither guy knows about the other." I want to sob, but I don't.

She's down the hall. I'm right behind her. I feel like I did when I was three years old, running after her for a hug and she was chasing Zach. Something burns in my throat.

"That's one of them out there right now. And the other one brings me home to this empty house. With his sister. She's called before. You've spoken to her. Lili."

Mom's at the front door.

"Taylor's pretty good-looking. Remember him? Zach's best friend? Check him out when you leave."

She opens the door and walks away from me to her car, and I feel like screaming I want to scream at her tackle her knock her to the ground make her love me again but instead I say, "I'm having sex with them both," then turn around and walk back inside to get my school things, after throwing a wave and smile at Jesse! Not Taylor! who comes toward the front door.

Gosh, I hope he didn't hear me.
Did he?
How loud was my voice?

Why did I say I was sleeping with Taylor *and* Jesse?
Why did I say it in front of people?
My heart pounds in my throat.

Does my mother care?
Did it bother her?

It must have affected her a little, or she wouldn't have
run like that.

Except,
except she could have run just because she hates me

so

much.

I had no idea.
Like she had no idea.
How could we know?

But *they* were fighting with him, not me.
He'd gotten someone pregnant. I hadn't.
He had depression. They knew.

It wasn't about me.

But that's what it's become.

I have to do a lot of deep breathing before I can step outside.
I stand in the dining room, look toward the foyer, wonder if I can make it to my book bag and then out the door and then to school and then back home again before cracking wide open.

"She doesn't get the control," I say to the light over the table. "Or the power. She doesn't run me anymore. I get to choose." But the words don't free me. In fact, I wonder if I'll even be able to stop crying.

So I stand there. Try to breathe. Try to stop weeping. Try not to be horrified. And when the knock comes, I let out a yelp of surprise. I can't go to the door, can't say anything; I wait, trembling, hoping for a miracle.

The front door opens a bit and Jesse sticks his head inside, and there we are, looking at each other, and I had forgotten they were coming to get me. That Taylor traded shifts. Like I'm a job. I feel that way again now.

Jesse doesn't say anything like, "Are you ready to go?" or, "We're gonna be late." He just walks inside, closing the door behind him, and it's so dark in here, and watery like the ocean too. No, those are my tears, and that's why I have the upside-down-in-the-salt-water feel.

I'm rooted between the foyer and the dining room, maybe sprouting leaves now. My books are steps away, and Jesse is so tall coming across the room like that. "Sex with two guys?" he says, and he has this funny look on his face, like he's not sure if he should laugh or not, or maybe he's disgusted with me, because I sure am. Then he has his arms around me.

We stand there, his arms tight, and I haven't moved still and I can't move until Mom is back inside, screaming.

She never says a word to me, even in her fury. Just hollers at Jesse, a kid she's never spoken to before. "Get the hell out of here. And take this piece of trash with you."
"You make me sick with your promiscuity."
"I'll call the police if you don't leave."

Like that, I'm free. I can move.

That thing Jesus says about how the truth shall set you free? Guess what? It's Mom's lies that make me free, make me move, grab my books, leave the room. Jesse's saying something (to me? to my mom?), then taking my hand, pulling me along.

I bump into a chair, bump into the doorknob. Jesse keeps walking, running his mouth, his words coming out fast and loud. I glance at his face, see that's he's mad—and remember Zach.

It was before Zacheus went to bed.

Taylor had been over, trying to see me, and I wouldn't have any of it because it felt like bad things were getting ready to happen. Our house was like a pot of boiling water overflowing.

"Come on, London,"Taylor said. "We need to talk."
"I can't," I had said. "Things are going on with Zach and Rachel. I kinda need to help out." I stood on the porch, blocking the front door. It was hot and humid and the mosquitoes were so thick you could almost hear them buzzing as a group. Inside the house Zach was swearing, Mom was hollering, and there was the rumble of my daddy trying to smooth things over.

My arms were folded, and I wondered if Taylor could hear them? How could he not? All that was going on inside. "It's not a good time for me right now."

Taylor hardly let those words come out of my mouth. "What about me, London?" He'd said that right in my face. Too close. I felt his breath on my skin. "What about us?"

There was a crashing noise—I can't remember what

broke now—but I looked at Taylor and said, "Are you kidding me? Can't you hear what's going on? *This* is what I have to do." Then I went inside.

Later I figured out Heather had been asking Taylor to do things. I mean, I saw them together at school the very next day. And Zach told me he'd beat the crap out of his friend if I needed him to. He wouldn't have said that, I realized later, if things weren't so bad between him and Rachel.

But that night, when I walked in the house, I saw it had become a war zone. Mom had broken several household items, and Daddy was trying to calm her. Zach was livid. At this point he thought he'd marry Rachel. That they'd take their baby and do the *Teen Mom* thing. It never occurred to him that Rachel would let her parents convince her of an abortion.

The deal is, Zach didn't get mad often.
He got sad.
But that day.
That day, as Taylor drove away from the house, Mom called Rachel a whore. And that was it.

"She's a whore. A slut. A Jezebel," Mom said.
"Mom." That was me. Those words coming out of her

mouth, and about wonderful Rachel—I would have laughed if I hadn't seen Zach's face change. It was all so bizarre. Daddy must have seen the change too, because he stepped in between my brother and mother.

"Zachy," I yelled.

But my brother seemed to hear nothing but the name-calling. He knocked our dad aside. Knocked him to the floor. And he was on Mom in a moment. Had her by the shoulders. Pushed her to the wall. Said, "I have had enough of you, Mom. You've done enough. Shut the hell up. Don't you ever say anything like that again."

"You're hurting me, Zacheus Lee Castle. Remove your hands from my person right now."

I hurried from Daddy's side, moving across the room. Tried to get to my brother. Daddy stood too.

"I'm done talking to you," Zach said. "I'll not speak another word to you the rest of my life."

Mom laughed, but I saw the look on her face. The gauntlet had been thrown down. "You won't talk to me?" she said, and laughed again.

I reached out for Zach, touched his arm. He looked at

me, and his eyes filled with tears, his face splotchy from anger. "You tell her, London," he said, his voice almost a whisper. "Tell her I'm done."

I was caught there in the middle. Daddy stood behind me.

"Tell her."

"He said, Mom . . . ," I said, faltering, not wanting to say anything at all, but Mom was too fast. "Don't *either* of you speak to me," she said.

And Zacheus didn't. Not even one more time. Not the rest of his life.

"Okay, wow," Jesse says. He still has my hand. "Wow."
He pulls me to the van. Lauren looks out the window—
what's she doing here?—and she isn't happy. Then she
must see my face, because she opens the door and
so does Lili and they jump out and run to meet us. All
three of them stand around me.

Tears keep running down my face, and I feel like perhaps
something has broken. Nothing as clichéd as my heart.
That broke months ago, anyway. I think maybe my eyes
have a malfunction or something.

What's weird is that the weather has changed overnight.
It's warm this morning.

"What is it?" Lili says, and her arms are around me,
and Lauren is petting Jesse, who says, "I've never seen
anything like that in real life."
"What?"
"Her mom. Her mom is messed up."

Messed up? My mother? Of course. Of course she is.
"I can take my brother's car," I say. I have the keys in my
bag. I dig around for them. "I want to be alone." I try to
say the words, but nothing comes out but *alone*.

261

"Oh, London," Lili says, and she hugs me close. "Come with us."

"Get the hell out of here!" The last word screams up, high, higher, and I'm sure that if I were to look in the cloudless sky, I'd see the last sounds of my mother there, proving she hates me.

We all turn and there she is. On the porch. Looking so beautiful but so . . . so angry. My mother. "Take her away. Get off my property."

My eyes are still broken and I can't quite walk, but I head toward Zach's car, and Jesse throws the keys to Lauren. "Drive the van," he says. And she doesn't even argue.

I follow the van for a bit, fall behind in school traffic,
almost hit a pedestrian, and pull over so I can cry. I rest
my head on the steering wheel.

"You okay, London?" Jesse says after a couple of minutes
of listening to me sob.
No. No, I'm not okay. I'm hurt. Embarrassed. And alone in
a family that should be holding each other up, not pushing
each other aside. I can't say any of this, though.

"You want me to drive?"
I nod.
"You want to go to school?"
I shake my head no.
"Want to go to the beach? I've always wanted to play
hooky at the beach. Can't do that in Utah."
"Sure," I say.

We change places, and I lean my head back and let the
tears leak from my broken eyes.

Jesse's silent. He takes the keys, adjusts the seat, hands
me a napkin from McDonald's (where'd that come
from?), and turns the car around.

We drive toward Ponce Inlet, a few miles up the coast. We drive slow, then look for a place to park.

I feel glued to the seat. The sun shines in nice and warm, but I'm a statue almost. And I should be, because I know how things are at home and why didn't I think that the rest of my world would find out how I live now?

It's warming up quick outside. I roll down the window, hoping for a breeze, but there's hardly anything out here now, which makes the air seem even warmer.

We're quiet. Jesse takes the keys from the ignition, hands them to me.
I want to look at him, but I can't.

This is all my fault.
I didn't have to push her.

But the thing is—the thing is, I *did*. I *had* to know she knew I'm still alive.

Jesse touches my hand. He's turned, looking at me.
"That's the weirdest thing I have ever seen," he says.

It seems he's careful with his words. Does he want to say, "Freak? Crazy? Mental?" I guess not, because he says, "Tell me what happened," as he shifts around in the seat, moving to face me more.

I look him right in the eyeball, and like that, I'm laughing. Laughing hard. But the laughing turns to wails. "I'm all alone. My brother's gone. Gone! And my mother hates me."

I shouldn't have gone after her. I regret that I did. But I'm sort of glad that I did too. "I'm all alone." My words are ragged. Broken. I roll the window the rest of the way down. Try to stop crying.

"Why does she think we're sleeping together?"

If this were any other life, I'd be laughing again. There'd be no tears. Instead, I look out at the ocean. The sun has made a mirror of the water. But the crash of the surf—it's so calming. I open the door. Kick off my shoes right there in the sand. I'm glad I wore a skirt today.

Walk. Walk, London Castle. The sand is warm, and the weather is getting more Florida-ish. I can't wait for the humidity. Jesse follows. He puts his hand in the middle of my back, like Jesus did so long ago after that village died, and when I glance over my shoulder at him, I see he looks like Jesus with his dark hair, dark eyes—if I squint just right.

"I told her," I say when I'm in the wet sand, his hand still there on my back, so warm. "I told her we're sexually active." I say this like it's a joke, but the sound of the words shows me nothing is funny. "I told her I've been doing it with more than one guy. You and my friend Taylor. And anyone else I can think of at school, for that matter. Including that one guy who sweats so much in our English class. You know who I mean?"

We're ankle deep in the water now. It's cold. I sit down. Lie back. Arms out. Ankles crossed. Eyes closed. Let the waves try to crash over me. I'm half wet, and I know it

266

won't be long before my clothes are full of sand and I'll be freezing, but I don't care.

"Yeah, I know who you mean," Jesse says, and he plops down next to me sitting. "He's kinda gross."

Even sweaters need love, I want to say, but the cold water feels too good and it's caressing the sides of my face, filling my ears, this calm crash of the ocean.

The night before he died, I made a pallet on Zach's floor.

Things were bad by then, but Mom refused to see, and when I said something to Daddy, he said, "Zach and your mom always fight like this."

And I had said, "Yes, this is more than Mom, Daddy. Rachel's gone too. I think he needs help."

We all knew about the abortion, but no one, no one in the family could say the word.

That night the sun was gone and the curtains on Zach's window blocked out the bits of stars. The room smelled sour, but I had been in there long enough I was used to it. I knew Zach was awake. I could tell by his breathing and the way he tossed and turned.

"We should go to the beach," I said. "Right now. You and me. Sneak out and go to the beach."

My brother didn't answer.

I've thought what we would have done if we'd gone that night.

It would have been way late, way late, like three in the morning, and we would have snuck out and driven to the beach. We'd have taken only our bathing suits, towels, and money for something at the 7-Eleven afterward.
The moon would have been high in the sky, and everything would have seemed like a midnight photograph, all purple-blues and grays, and even the suds coming upon the shore would have held color.

There would have been no sharks, no jellyfish, no Mom. No dead babies, no sadness, no man-o-war.

Just me and my brother.
Just my brother and me.
Out in the water.
Happy.

"We heard him dying," I say.

It's the third time I've said it.
I screamed it first to my father when he came running in
the door and we had already cut Zach down and Mom
had gotten his heart beating again
said it a second time to the police when they
questioned me and my eyes were so swollen I could
almost not open them
and this is the third time right now with the ocean trying
to soothe me with salt and sand and foam that crackles
in my ears.

"What?"

I can tell Jesse understood me, so I don't repeat it. The
words burn my mouth anyway. Overhead, the sun seems
determined to toast my eyelids. But that's okay, because
maybe I will never leave this place.

"Did you know shark attacks can happen in less than
knee-deep water?"
Jesse's silent.
"Did you know that my daddy spoke at a funeral for a
family with nine children. The youngest got electrocuted
by a hair dryer. A little girl. Me and Zach, we were

270

heartbroken. They still go to church with us."

I'm sinking in the sand, but I'm okay with it right now too. I've already tested the theory and you can't sink to China.

(I would have tried to that night with my brother, Zacheus, too.)

"Did you know you can make soup from the periwinkles out here? They're so beautiful."

Jesse doesn't say a thing. Just sits there with me, and when I look at him, finally, there's a halo of light around his head.

Jesse lies down next to me. He takes my hand in his. His fingers are warm.

"My brother was my very best friend," I say. "You two remind me of us."
"Who?"
"You and Lili remind me of Zach and me. Together."
Waves crash. Water rushes up around us. I turn my head a bit and taste saltwater. "Is Lili your best friend?"

Jesse's quiet. "My youngest brother is. Nate?"
I nod. Natey.
"When he was born, that was the best thing that had ever happened to me. I knew we'd be best friends right at that moment."
I look at the sky. So blue. So blue.
"But me and Lili? We're close."

I don't know how long I lie there, but when I finally stand up, I'm so covered in sand—and wet top to bottom—that I have to walk down the beach until I can find a shower.

"I'll try to drip-dry before we get in the car," I say.
I face the sun. *Keep coming, hot weather. Keep coming.*
Out in the water, I see two people kiteboarding, their

kites (one yellow and one red) pulling them along through the waves.

My hair slaps heavy and sandy at my back. I itch from the salt and sand.

"I should know this," Jesse says. "But why did you tell her that we're together?"

I open my mouth again. "To feel alive."

He nods like that's an answer he understands. He laces his fingers through mine.

"We're a secret," I say. "Nothing to anyone—not even Taylor or Lauren. Not even Lili or Nathan."

"I can do that," Jesse says.

In the outdoor shower, the wind blowing sand against my damp legs, Jesse kisses me, the water running down my face. He kisses my eyes, wipes the sun from my forehead, whispers words with that Utah accent. "You're alive, London."

We stay gone until it's time for Jesse to meet Lili at school.

I drop him off because I'm afraid Lili will know I kissed her brother, and even though she was encouraging it, she may not like it because she knows about Taylor.

I know about Taylor.

What am I doing?

I can't help it.

I've gone crazy.

First I pushed my mother over the edge and I let her push me over the edge, though the truth is, Mom has nothing to do with my cheating.

How is Taylor different from Jesse?
Taller.
A little more muscle-y.
Blond.
Soft-spoken.

But, the thing is, I need saving.
And maybe this stranger can do it.
And I can hold Taylor close too,
figure myself out.

Because nobody has to tell me, I'm all messed up.

An accident you're in? It marks you on the outside,
maybe. Scars your face or your skin—breaks bones,
crushes skulls, leaves the body changed.

An accident witnessed? You're different on the inside.
Maybe there's no cut someone else can see, but there're
always injuries on the inside.
Those take a long time to heal.

My mother and father, their wounds are huge, gaping,
they drip—ooze. Their battle is with me, too, when I
should be close to them, on their side.
That's what I want.
To be with them.

Mom hasn't touched me like a mom should, not once,
since we found Zach.

Maybe I'll never get better from Zach's leaving us.
Maybe I'll carry all that around with me forever,
hearing him, finding him,
moving too slow,
moving way too s l o w.

Maybe my curse will be memory forever.

Maybe what I'm going through
maybe all this I feel
maybe it *is* part of repentance
saying I'm sorry
for not moving faster, opening the door faster, clawing
my way to Zachy faster.

God knows I'm sorry.
Jesus knows I'm sorry.
No one
no one could be sorrier than I am.
I stand on my own Golgotha and I'm all alone.

There's a message from Rachel when I get home. "Hey, London. I'm calling you back. I've . . . I'm so glad you called. I've got stuff to tell you. We need to catch up. I can't wait to talk to you."

For a minute—no, for lots of minutes, for hours, days, weeks, I hated (still hate?) Rachel for living and moving when everyone else got stuck here in this awful place called my home.
But I think, I think
I can go on now, now that I've heard her voice on our answering machine.
My brother would want me to.

Still, I'm scared. Scared that we're almost communicating.

I mean, we are, right? Sort of?

And I want to, right? Yes, no, maybe so.

Am I five? Oh, I wish I were.

I shower again. Wash sand from my ears. Hear those words, "We need to catch up."
Try to think how to save the call but keep Daddy and Mom from hearing it.
Wonder at Taylor.
Think of Jesse kissing me in that cool water as I tried to rinse the beach from my skin.

I get out of the shower, wrap in my terry-cloth bathrobe, lie down on my bed just to rest my eyelids, which are sunburned

after all.

"Hey, London," Zach says. He touches me. His hands are cold, way cold, and I push him away.

"What?"

He grins at me big. His eyes go squinty, disappearing. "I need you to do me a favor."

I sit up, pulling the bathrobe tight, cinching the pink sash. My room is dim. I can hear someone in the house. Who's come home?
Did they check on me while I was sleeping?

Daddy calls to Mom, "Eva, I've got the dressing for the salad." Mom says, "Tell that daughter of yours to get up. We have work to do."

"Did you hear that?" I say to Zach. "Mom mentioned me to Daddy." I get to my knees.

"You're dreaming," Zach says. His breath is ice. "Listen to me. Look at me, London. Me. You need to choose."

Choose? I can't look at him. I don't know why. I try to. But I want to see that my mother isn't mad anymore. I want to go to my mother, see if she'll wrap her arms around me, kiss my face, touch my hair, pet away a sadness that I feel growing within.

"If you don't pay attention," Zach says, "I have to go."

My eyes burn. There's salt water in them. And sand, too, maybe. He lets out a huge sigh. He touches my hand and he's so cold. I want to say, "Heaven's full of gold and light, right? So why are you cold?" I try to look at him, but now his face is too bright, and I squint too, like his smiley eyes.

"I would have named my daughter London," he says, letting out a little laugh. "After you, sis." And he's gone with a second sigh.

When I open my eyes, the house is dead quiet.
I lie there, tears leaking toward my ears.
My nose goes snuffy.

I remember Jesus.
He cried for Mary and Martha.
He cried when Lazarus died.

Has He cried for me?

I get up, moving slow, and start to get dressed for evening at my house.

"This will be so much fun," I say, dropping my bathrobe at my feet and walking to the St. Ives lotion. I slather it everywhere, standing in front of the mirror.

I'm losing weight. Still. The doctor said no more. But I can't help it. Food is tasteless. "It would have flavor if Mom would eat with us." And I know, soon as I say the words, what I'm saying is true. The only thing big on me anymore is my hair. It feels like a cape on my back, around my shoulders. And because I didn't brush it or braid it or anything before I lay down, it's frizzy. "I don't care."

When the lotion has soaked into my thirsty skin, I dress. Then I pack a bag. I'm having a sleepover tonight.

The front door closes and I hear Mom and Daddy—both home now (was Mom all along? Was he? Did they walk in together?)—voices low.

"Screw them," I say. My hands shake as I put a set of jammies and tomorrow's school clothes and a hairbrush and toothbrush and makeup in a bag. Underwear, different bra, schoolbooks. "What else do I need?"

Something for breakfast.

Attention.
My parents.
Zach back.
Two boys kissing me at once.
Rachel's voice talking in my ear.
My brother, alive.
Someone at home talking to me.

My legs shake as I walk, down the hall to the family room. Mom sits in her chair, Zach's baby book closed on her knees. Daddy looks up from the newspaper.

"Wild Thing," he says when he sees me. He gives me a sort-of smile. My heart leaps a bit, and I touch my hair. He hasn't called me that in a forever. He folds the paper, sets it aside. "We were talking about pizza for dinner tonight."

I see Daddy not looking at my mother. So I do look. She stares out curtained windows. Her hands are fists. She hates me so much.

"Your mother isn't hungry, though, so it'll just be us."

Dinner with my daddy.

He stands, not waiting to hear my answer, sees the bag in my hands. "Were you going somewhere?"

"I thought"—I have to clear my throat to pull out the words—"I thought I'd have a sleepover somewhere."

"Whose house?"

I can hear the clock on the mantel. Smell my mother's Shalimar. Feel the dryness of the bag in my hand. The weight of my books. My feet on the terrazzo floor. The way she looks away. I feel it all at once. "I hadn't decided."

Daddy comes to me, hesitates, runs his hand down his face like he is trying to change the shape. "Not tonight, Wild Thing." His voice is low. "It's you and me tonight. Dinner and a movie."

Tears spring to my eyes. "Really?"
This could be a dream.
A trick.

"Really," Daddy says, and he starts to come to life.

So I _don't_ spend the night away.

I'm with Daddy. And while we don't talk about anything, words come out of our mouths. And when it's all said and done, he hugs me good night, in the darkness of the foyer.

"Sorry," he says.

He's not so tall and my head is next to his. "No," I say. "I wanted to hug."

"No, I mean about the other things."

"Oh," I say.

And when I head off to bed, it feels like I shed a second skin.

Choose.
What?
Who?

School has more colors the next day.

I'm more alive.

I refuse to think anything but good thoughts, and when Taylor comes to the door to get me, not even beeping, I link my arm with his.

"Hey," he says, and his face is surprised.

"Hey, what?" Can Mom see us from her bedroom? *Don't think that. You don't care. I do. You don't.* I get in the car, sit in the seat my brother sat in for so many years (*Think only of yourself today, no Zacheus Lee Castle. Only London Marie Castle.*), watch Taylor walk around the front of the car.

The morning sun slides at him sideways, and it seems his hair is blonder than usual. He looks at me through the glass and I can see I've made him nervous, and for some reason, that is so hot I can't stand it. He's not even shut the door when I crawl over the emergency brake to kiss him.

It's a long, happy kiss. One that makes me lose my breath.

"Wow. Okay. Thanks," he says when I pull away. His hand is on my waist, under my shirt a bit.

No more Jesse, maybe, I think as I look toward the house then give the blind windows the finger just in case Mom's home.

School has a different thought for me.

I don't share classes with Taylor, and during lunch, Lili chatting ninety miles per hour, three boys, and one girl come up to the table where Lauren has plopped down too. She doesn't share a lunch with Jesse.

"So when I get home, I see all the sand. I knew you two went to the beach." Lili doesn't stop talking.

"Is that where he was?" Lauren says. She looks a bit unhappy between the eyebrows.

"I couldn't do school," I say. One of the guys looks at me, and I recognize him from football. In fact, Zach was on the team with all three of these fellows. The redhead has a barracuda shaved into his buzz cut.

"It's been a while now," one guy says, and I realize he's talking to me.

What?

"Since Zach died. I never got to say I was sorry, London. I liked your brother. Everyone did. He was a good tight end."

Redhead nods and the third guy just eats.

But the girl, she's a cheerleader, she says, "I heard you cut him down. That you heard him trying to kick free of the rope."

Take a breath.
"What?"

"I heard that you're the one who tried to save him. That you could hear him kicking at the walls and stuff. Is that true?"

I can't swallow.

Lili's gone quiet and Lauren scoots her chair back. The room has gone black and white and my ears ring like someone slapped me hard. It takes less than ten seconds for this girl I don't know to tell my brother's life story. I mean, his death story.

Everyone's looking at me except Lili, who spears lettuce leaves over and over.

"Yes," I say.

"I heard you brought him back to life with CPR but there was too much damage and so you had to pull the plug."

Umm.

"Shut up!" Lauren says. She screams it. "Shut up! Shut up!"

This girl's spoken the truth about the most important seconds of my life. I look around the room. Man, my head hurts.

"I'd better go," I say. And Lili says, "London." The lunchroom has quieted, some kids watch us.

"You're an idiot," Lauren says. She's still screaming. "He was someone's brother and son and my friend." Her voice cracks and I see she liked my brother a lot. A way lot. But I look at it all like I'm seeing through the lens of a camera. I'm seeing it all at a distance. Floating above it.

Where's Jesse? I think. Or Taylor? If I could get away from here.
You always run.
I always run. It's easiest that way.
Find someone to hide with.
Look the other direction.
Wish he hadn't hanged himself.

I'm running.

To Taylor's class.
Someone's screaming Zach's name and it could be me,
but maybe it's Lili or Lauren, who follow behind.
"It's true," I say when one of them touches me. "It's true.
We couldn't save him. And we tried. We both tried."
The bell rings and the hall fills with people. Taylor will
be out of the class in a moment and I'll go home. Now.
Now. Now.

"I heard him," I say. My voice is shrill, but it's coming out
of me like water from a broken fountain. "I heard him
kicking and I didn't go that second. I thought he was
mad. They'd been fighting. She'd been on his back." A big
guy knocks into me. My books spill to the floor. Lili goes
for them.

"But I waited. I waited a few seconds."

"You don't have to say anything," Lauren says. "We don't
care." She's crying. She must have really liked Zach to cry
in the hall like this.
The thought comes that she must really like me, too.
Still.

My mouth won't stop. There's hurt dammed up inside
me, maybe behind the words. "And I didn't get there in

time!" A couple of people turn, stare. "I didn't get there in time. I didn't save him. And Mom held him under his arms. Tried to keep him off his neck and I cut the rope."

Taylor's there all the sudden. "London!" His hands are on me.

"But we couldn't get it off in time. We tried. But we couldn't. And then we did and . . ." This part of the story is a scream. "And now she won't talk to me!"

A teacher is in the hall. And another. There's Jesse. He's running toward us and I shove my way through the crowd, people grabbing at me. And maybe I am the woman caught in adultery. Or the woman with an issue of blood. If I could get to Jesus—I mean Jesse—if I could get to them both, I would be fine.

I put my hands on his face. "Take me home," I say.

And he does.

Here's the deal.
I'm sleep-talking. Like, my eyes are closed and my mouth
is going.

In the parking lot Taylor said, "Take her. Save her. Get her
home."
He sounded so sad.
(Did he know about me kissing Jesse?
Would he care?)
And Lauren was crying and Lili said, "I think she needs a
doctor."
But all I need is to sleep-talk.

"She hasn't spoken to me in almost a year," I say to Jesse.
My head's in his lap. My knees are bent on the seat. The
buckle from the seat belt jabs at my hip but I don't care.
I deserve pain. One of Jesse's hands is tangled in my hair.

"I wish you had known my Zachy."
"She had an abortion."
"We did our best. I swear to all that's holy, we did our
best."

The van bounces to a stop.
Outside I can hear a mockingbird call.

In my head is my mother screaming that I should have done more. I should have done more.

Busted that door down.

He's dead because I didn't do more.

"Do you believe in Jesus?"

Jesse looks at me so brown-eyed it hurts. He nods. "I do," he says.

I sit up.

"I think you look like him."

Jesse looks startled. He almost smiles. Clears his throat. "I don't think so," he says.

I take a deep breath. "Would you care if I called you Jesus?"

"What?" He grips the steering wheel with one hand. His other has slipped from my hair to the seat.

"I'm being weird," I say. "I know that." But I can't stop. Panic is caught in my throat. I shouldn't have talked about anything that happened. Why did I do that at school? It wasn't my fault. It's been a sort-of secret that everyone knows but that I never speak of. It was that cheerleader. "If you let me, I would be sitting next to Jesus right this very second." My heart's beating too fast.

"Jesse's good." He looks a little freaked out.

I just stare at Jesse and he looks back and then, after a moment, he kisses me. I put my hands to his face and

I wonder if Jesus is okay with me kissing two guys and that my mom doesn't talk to me and that my brother is dead. It's a long kiss, a kiss where I want to get closer to Jesse but I can't because we're in the van and there's a steering wheel.

"We should go inside," I say.

He doesn't say anything, just follows me. Mom's gone, and I'm relieved because I don't have to fake anything or be anything or pretend like she cares. I just want to sit with this boy, sit next to this Jesus-looking boy, and kiss him and let him slide his hands through my hair, and I want to touch his neck, put both my hands around it— feel the pulse of his life beneath my fingers.

In the house, I remember it all over again.
Mom screaming. Daddy reaching for her, but she slaps
his hands away, and I want to slap her and Daddy and
Zacheus for doing this to himself
to us.

"He's gone," Daddy says. We're in Zach's hospital room.
"We have to let him go." Daddy's voice is near the
wheels of the bed, next to that shiny floor.

"No, he isn't!" Mom screams. "We got to him in time.
We did!"

She points at me—at me—like I'm the one who did it.
Like I'm the one who put something around my neck
and choked off my own air.
What did my brother think,
locking the door like that?

What did he think? That I could bust doors down, that I
could lift him as much as he weighed
and the shoe marks on the walls
and I tried.
I tried to help him.
We both did.

The room is sterile and white and I love my brother,
lying on the bed, I love my mother and father and my
brother. My best friend.

I don't say anything, though. I watch my mother and
when she lets out that final wail I move to her.

"Mommy," I say, but she is so angry—so angry.

"You!" she says. "You could have saved him. You were there."

I blink. Stop. Wait. "We were both there."

"But you were first."

I want to say, I tried. I want to say, I tried, Mom. The nurse comes in the room, asks Mom to quiet down, and I think Mom might shoot that woman's eyes out.

Daddy is after Mom now, his arms tight, pinning her
but she struggles
she gets free and she's at me, the nurse watching, my
mother pointing, her nail so polished, so shiny, I can
almost smell the color.
"You!" she says, and slaps me so hard that I stagger to
stay on my feet and at first I feel nothing but the sound
and *then* there's the burn.

Daddy raises his voice
and the whole family is coming apart at the seams
like a fabric that should have held together but couldn't
all because of one choice.

I touch my face, it's burning now, and then I run to the
waiting room because I can't go farther than that.

Run as fast as I can out of there
out of there
out of there

And wait.

Because he's gone for good and we have to let him go
a broken family.

I remember this all in the foyer, walking down the hall through the dining room to the living room.

"Let's kiss in here, Jesse," I say.

"I should go back to school," he says, but he's sliding his arms around me and pulling me close, and I think of Taylor in the waiting room, see that he's been crying, then press my mouth to Jesse and try to erase everything anything all of it every bit of my brother's death—something I can't do with Taylor.

If my mother were to see me now.
What would she think?
My hands on him, his on me.
Cleave unto your spouse, I think, and I laugh midkiss, my
palms under Jesse's shirt. His skin is so smooth. He's so
warm.

Where are Mom and Dad?
I lead Jesse into the family room, where I used to watch
The Office reruns with Zach and Rachel and Taylor.
We sit next to each other and I don't know why but
while we're kissing I start crying.
I mean, I don't make a sound or anything, but the tears
run down my face.

Jesse moves away a bit, looks at me. Runs his thumbs
across my cheeks. "Oh, London," he says. "Your heart is
broken, isn't it?"

"Yes," I say.

And even though I want him to kiss me more and more
and more, he just wraps his arms around me and pulls
me close.

No sex.

If my mother knew how he saved me, she'd fold up on herself. Maybe tear her eyes away from my brother's memory long enough to shout her disgust.

No sex.
But I could go there, would go there, if he asked me
if he said it would save me
would keep me here
make my mother notice me again.

I don't tell him any of that. I just weep, his arms around me until Lili and Lauren and Taylor arrive, walking into the house without even waiting for me to say, "Come in."

I talk to them about the end with my brother.

The hanging
Him kicking the wall as he struggled before we got in
there
how I heard him and didn't know at first
just thought he was mad because of the fight
had no idea
and then somehow, somehow KNEW I should hurry
hurry hurry
get in there
screaming for Mom
the kicking getting less
trying to get the door open
hitting it
hitting
it splintering.
Mom arguing with me
how we tried so hard to save him
Daddy taking over
the EMTs

My poor brother, never regaining consciousness.

And then the blaming,

the slap,
the screaming,
the silence.

My own death here
in this house too,
and I'm not even sure
why.

"I tried to make him live," I say to them all. Lauren is
crying and so is Lili. Taylor looks out the window the
whole time I talk.
Jesse still holds me but his arms are loose and I think of
Jesus's arms and how I need Him, *that's* who I need and
I know I know Him through these friends but that I'm
going to have to keep following Him to keep whole.

They stay for hours.

And I want them to live with me, all of them, petting me
and touching my hair and letting me cry and talk and
hugging me and all that. Something I haven't gotten in so
long.

Daddy comes home and when he walks in the family
room we all look at him and he looks at us and then he
says, "Have you been remembering my son?"

Lauren rushes to him and hugs him. She's not crying
anymore but I can tell she's close to tears.

Daddy stands there, still, then puts his arms around her.

"He was great," Lauren says. "No. He *is* great."

Lili says, "And so is London. She's the best friend I've
ever had." Her words are a surprise.

She looks at her brother. "She needs you." And I can't
tell if she's talking to Daddy or Jesse. Jesse runs his hand
over my shoulder. Then Lili says, "We have to go home."
She almost smiles. "Or Mom's going to have a miocardial
infarction."

Everyone stands to go and right at that moment I
hear Mom come into the house. Daddy looks over his
shoulder and his eyebrows knit together. Is he scared of
her too? Or of what might come?

Mom is in the room, and it's like we all take a breath.
She steps forward when we inhale, it seems, staggers
a moment, looks at Daddy and then at the boys in the
room. She sees Lauren, raises her eyebrows. Her face
grows hard. I can see she's had her nails done. She never
once looks at me.

"Allen, you know I don't like company when I'm not
warned."
Her voice is a sheet of ice. Her words slide down
toward us, land in a pile in the front of the group.

Lauren straightens her back. I bet she gets three inches
taller. Does she remember when she was caught with
Zach? Of course she does. She opens her mouth to
speak, and my words seem to come from her mouth.

"These are *my* friends," I say. "They're here for me."
"Get out," Mom says, and she doesn't look in my direction.
Nine months' practice, she doesn't even glance at me.
"No!" My voice comes out louder than I intend. "They're
here for me."
I see Lili move a little. Start. She's uncomfortable, I can
tell. Even though she stood to go, Lili sits back down and
then pats the sofa. "Jesse," she says. Her voice is weak.

313

"I think," Daddy says.

"No!" I say again, and my voice is louder this time. "No! I have friends. I'm here still. I'm not dead. Zach is dead. I'm here."

That gets my mother. I can tell. There's penetration. My words have struck a mark. Still she says nothing, doesn't look at me. She lowers her voice like a bull getting ready to charge. "Leave. My. Home."

"Kids," Daddy says. "I think it's best. . . ."

I'm not sure how it happens, but I move from where I am near Jesse to Mom. I almost fall, tripping over someone's feet. Lauren grabs me. I thought she hated me. No, I hated her. No, I hate my mom.

"I begged for you to help me," I say.
The Death is there. In the room with us. On my lips. We've been talking about it so it's uncovered from where I've kept it hidden.
"I called you. Called you."
Mom looks at me.
"He was alive. And I begged you to help me. We could hear him."

"Shut up." Mom's voice is a whisper.

"I called for you and you said he's just throwing a tantrum, and I said, 'Help me, something's wrong in there.' And by the time you came with that key, it was too late. He wasn't alive anymore."

"Shut up!"

"If you would have listened! If you would have helped."

"Shut up!"

"You needed someone to blame and you chose me."

"Shut up!"

"It wasn't me, Mom! I didn't kill Zacheus. He killed himself."

Mom slaps me, hard.

Lili lets out a cry.

Daddy moves and Taylor leaps near me.

I put my hand out, touch my face where it burns, lean at my mother. When I speak, I'm screaming. "I did the best I could. And I'm here, alive." My voice soars toward the ceiling. I want to grab her, shake her, make her understand. "I still love you! Please love me back." I almost can't get the words out, I'm crying that hard.

Mom leans so close I can smell her lipstick. Between clenched teeth she says, "I quit loving everyone the day my son died. And that includes you."

315

Her words are a fist to my gut.

"Eva," Daddy says. "Oh, Eva."

"I'm done," Mom says. "I'm done with all this." She leaves then. Goes to the room she shares with Daddy.

And I'm left alone.

No!
Not alone.
Not this time.

Alone.

Mom packs. Daddy goes in to her. I can hear him talking, his voice soothing and then rising in desperation.

"We'd better go," Lauren says, and Lili nods.
Lauren comes close, puts her arms around me tight.
"Your brother was my first real heartbreak," she says.
She presses her lips to my cheek where my mother slapped me. "I'm so glad he was my first true love."

Lili hugs me next. Her eyes are shiny with tears. "London, you're a great friend," she says, and she hugs me so tight she squeezes the breath out of my lungs.

Jesse says nothing. Just puts an arm back around me, and when we look each other in the eye we know we were close to being caught and I think, *I'm done with that.* And maybe he thinks, *Yes, me too.*

I walk everyone to the door. My feet feel like they have grown way too big, and I trip over nothing. Lili catches my arm. Holds my hand.

"It'll be okay," Taylor says. "I have this feeling."

Taylor puts his hand on my shoulder and this warmth moves right out of his fingertips and I realize, with that touch, I am going to heal. It's a fragile feeling and it makes my throat close up.

Behind me my parents have raised their voices. Taylor doesn't even blink at the sound. Just lets me know he's there.

"She won't be back," Daddy tells me lots later. "I couldn't stop her."

It's weird.

The house is less empty with my mother gone than it was when she lived here.

I turn my music on.

I help Daddy pack up some of Zachy's things.

We move a desk into the living room for Daddy to
write at.

Go to lunch.

Talk.

Laugh.

Late that night, though, I hear him crying.

He misses my mother.

I know.

But I can't say (is this evil?) that I do.

I've learned to live without her.

Three days after my mother leaves, the phone rings.
I know it's not her. She hasn't called at all—not that I've
seen.
As I walk to the phone, I wonder—has Daddy called
her?
Has she thought of us once?
Does she miss Zach more or less now that she's gone?

I pick up the phone, glance at caller ID. I don't recognize
who it is.

"Hello?"
"London?"
I know her. "Rachel," I whisper.
"Anyone there?" she says.
I speak louder. "Rachel," I say. "Hello!"
My hearts thumps.

"Hey!" She sounds so . . . happy. Like she hasn't been
fighting to get out of fog for that last almost-year. Or
maybe she has and she's succeeded.
Whatever, she sounds good.

"I'm back in town," she says. "I want to see you."
I nod, then find my voice though my fingertips have
gone numb. Before the words come out I think,

Why should I?
You left my brother.
He died because of you.
Murderer!
Why are you back?
Do you have any idea what we went through here?
Why now?
Why should I?

I swallow. "Okay, Rachel," I say. "Where?"

Time has this way of slowing down and speeding up, depending on how it feels.

When I'm kissing Taylor, time moves so fast I think I must age a million years in a few hot moments.

When Mom was home, in the same room with me, time didn't even pass. Seconds went on forever and I felt I might stop breathing for the pain of it all, and how long it seemed to take.

And when we found my brother, Zacheus, hanging in his room, time both sped up and slowed down. The way I ran and couldn't get to him fast enough and how Mom seemed to take her time trying to help and how long it was for the ambulance to get to us.

Time does this to me now. Slows down *and* speeds up. Rachel and I plan to meet late that afternoon, at the library.

I spend more energy changing clothes and thinking what's best to wear than I ever have when I wanted to impress any guy. The clock doesn't seem to move. The next thing I know, it's almost five p.m. and I have to run out the door to get to the library on time.

I sit in the parking lot for several minutes.
It's warm outside and sweat trickles down my forehead,
making my skin itch.

Will she recognize me?
Will I recognize her?
Will I slap her?
Cry?
Not show up?
Run?
Hide?
Drive away right now?
Maybe *she* won't come. Maybe this is all a trick.

I close my eyes and wish Zach were here with me. How
many times have I wished that very thing—a million? A
gajillion?

Oh, Zach, Zach.

Somehow, I get out of the car and walk around to the front of the library. Up the steps. Through the double doors, and there she is. Looking right at me. A baby in her arms.

I blink.
Am I imagining this? Is it her? Really?

I look behind me, I'm that confused, because maybe I have come to the wrong library here in New Smyrna Beach. Maybe that's not a baby. Maybe that's not Rachel but some unknown twin.

She steps forward, fast, and then Rachel's there, one arm going around my neck, and without meaning to, as soon as I see that baby's face and my brother's eyes, I burst into tears.

"There was no way," Rachel says as we settle down at a table in the children's section of the library, "that I was going to have an abortion."

"But that's what you told Zach."
She shakes her head. "I told him my mom and dad wanted that. Not that I would do it."

I swallow. "He thought. . . ." And I can't keep going.
She looks at me. Rachel's eyes are so clear I can tell she's telling the truth. Does she have any idea, ANY idea, that her words were the end for my brother?

"I kept telling him that I would work things out." She swallows and those clear eyes fill with tears. When she tries to speak, the words won't come out. She takes my hand. Pulls in air. "I loved him. I love him still. If I had known . . ."

And then, without my even asking, Rachel hands her daughter to me. My brother's daughter. My *niece*. "London," she says.

"Yes?" My voice is a whisper. I can't get over this baby's dark-lashed eyes. She looks so much like Zacheus I can't believe it. Even her little bald head is like Zach's when *he* was a baby.

"That's her name," Rachel says. "When I thought what to call her, I just knew Zach would want her named after you. Her middle name is Faith, for her father."
Faith, like my brother.

Now I can't speak. There's so much I want to say. But all I do is bring that baby to my lips and kiss her cheek, soft as air.

Maybe nothing could have saved Zach.
Maybe things were too messed up before he ever met
Rachel. Maybe he was too sad since we were little.
Maybe he had faith in everyone but himself.
Or . . .
Or maybe he just made a mistake and realized moments
too late.

After the library, the feel of London Faith still in my
arms, I climb in my brother's car
—it will always be his—and drive.

I drive straight to Taylor's house.

His car's in the driveway. I see that as I round the
corner.
My heart pounds so it makes me sick to my stomach.
What in the world? What am I scared about?

When I turn off the car and take the keys from the
ignition, I drop them my hand is trembling so and I leave
them on the floor mat. I have to swallow a couple of
times. Rest my head on the steering wheel. When I look
up, I see Taylor standing on his front porch, hands deep
in his pockets, the door ajar behind him.

He just stands there, waiting,
waiting for me.
Like he has for the last few months.

I get out of the car. At first I can't quite move my feet, and
then I can't get to him fast enough.

"London," he says when I'm standing in front of him.

I swallow. "I have a niece," I say. "A little girl niece."

This slow smile starts across Taylor's face. "A little girl niece?" he says. "She kept it?"

"Her. She kept *her.*"

And then I put both my hands on his face and kiss him. "Thank you," I say. "Thank you for waiting for me to come back."

I put my arms around him, my head on his chest, listen to his heart. After a second or two his hands rest on my hips, and we stand there like that for I don't know how long.

When I open my eyes, the moon has filled my bedroom with light.

Zach's at the foot of my bed. "You are hard to wake up."

"Zachy," I say. "I saw her."

He doesn't say anything, just kind of turns away from me. When he looks back, I can see he's crying. The tears slide down his face like diamonds.

"Is she pretty?" he says.

"Beautiful."

I can see my breath. I sit up, scoot down the bed till I sit right next to my brother. I kiss his cheek and his face is as soft as London Faith's. "She's just like you."

Zach shakes his head and tears fall in his lap, shining, diamond chips, then disappear.

"I'll do everything I can for her," I say.

"I know you will, London," Zach says. And then he sobs. "I miss you all so much," he says. "I miss you all so much."

I'm crying too. Crying like nothing could stop me. "I miss you too, Zach. We all do."

"She'll never know me," he says, and that makes me cry even harder.

"I'll tell her everything," I say.

"Everything?" he asks. He hesitates. "Even the end?"
I swallow. "When she's ready." My words come out like a puff of frozen steam.

"I love you, London," he says. "More than you can know."
And then he's gone,
and I awake with a start.

"London?"

Daddy stands in my room, just in the doorway. The moon is so bright I can see he wears striped pajamas. "You okay, London?"

I'm crying, hard. I have to grab at air to speak. "Yes."

Daddy pads into my room, and I see that he's put on his slippers.

He sits on the bed, exactly where Zach sat, and I pull the covers to my chin. We're quiet for a long time. Then I say, "I think we're going to make it, Daddy."

He lets out a sigh, bows his head like he's praying. "You think so, London?"

My throat closes up, but I manage to say, "Yes, Daddy, I do." I pull in a deep breath, hoping to Jesus, my good Jesus, that I am right. Then I whisper, "Let me tell you about his little girl."